DEATH IN A
PRIVATE GIRLS' SCHOOL

The shocking announcement sent a shudder of horror through staid Bramthorpe College. Only yesterday, the beautiful headmistress had been in perfect health and high spirits. Today she was dead—victim of a fatal poison.

Had a schoolgirl prank turned into a lethal game? Had her future in-laws decided to prune her from their family tree? Had a jealous rival taken revenge? Or had the lovely Miss Holland really taken her own life?

Everyone was stunned. There were tears in every eye. But one of the mourners smiled with the secret satisfaction of someone who was getting away with murder.

Murder Ink.® Mysteries

Scene of the Crime® Mysteries

A Murder Ink.® Mystery

GOLDEN RAIN

Douglas Clark

A DELL BOOK

Published by
Dell Publishing Co., Inc.
1 Dag Hammarskjold Plaza
New York, New York 10017

This work was first published in Great Britain
by Victor Gollancz Ltd.

Dell ® TM 681510, Dell Publishing Co., Inc.

ISBN: 0-440-12932-X

Printed in the United States of America
First U.S.A. printing—July 1982

CHAPTER I

The day began like any other at Bramthorpe College for Girls; always referred to simply as Bramthorpe, only ever being afforded its full title in the official lists of Principal Girls' Schools in reference books and almanacs.

The electric bells sounded throughout the building at a quarter to nine. At that precise moment two doors were opened. Day girls and boarders alike streamed through, directly into the cloakrooms to hang up coats and to change into houseshoes. In seemly fashion—no shouting or running in the corridors was permitted—the young ladies then made their way to their form rooms where monitors collected the exercise books containing the previous evening's written prep.

At ten to nine, the second bell sounded. By now the cloakrooms were empty, but just to make sure, the duty mistress of the week visited them, noting carefully any gross untidiness so that the culprits—easily identified by the numbers on the pegs—could be spoken to later. At the same time, the school prefects left their sanctum and went one to each form room. Their job was first, to ensure that the monitors had collected and counted the exercise books and then carried them to the open lockers outside the staff common room, there to be left for the mistresses concerned to collect

7

for marking. Second, to ensure that girls whose first lesson would be elsewhere than in their own form rooms collected from their desks the books that would be needed during the first period. Third, to ensure that every girl took from her desk her Bible and hymn book. Fourth, and finally, to make sure, as soon as the third bell sounded at five to nine, that girls left their form rooms, armed with all the necessary volumes, and made their way to Big Hall for Assembly.

It was all a routine, smooth and practised. Some forms had a long way to go to the hall. The next five minutes, however, allowed plenty of time. In the hall, waiting to receive them, was the duty mistress. Each girl filed to her allotted seat. The prefects sat down the left-hand gangway, each with the form for which she was responsible. While the duty mistress kept order, the prefects counted their charges and noted any empty seats. At two minutes to nine, the other mistresses filed in and up the stairs onto the stage. The one who accompanied the singing removed the all-enveloping dust-cover from the grand piano and took her seat at the instrument. The other mistresses sat down—being careful to remove their hymnals from the seats of their chairs before doing so.

But today there was a difference. The deputy headmistress, Miss Bulmer, did not enter with the rest of her colleagues. Her non-appearance was enough of an incident to cause comment in this well-ordered assembly.

"Where's the Bull?"

"The Bull's got collywobbles—I hope."

"Quiet. Samantha Ellison . . . and you, Sara Brett . . . you are talking." The duty mistress was picking out the culprits in her effort to quell the murmur of comment.

8

Nine o'clock. As the bells sounded, the hall door nearest the stage opened—as it always did—but not, this time, to admit the headmistress. In her stead came the missing Miss Bulmer.

"It's not the Bull who's ill. It's the Old Dutch."

"The Old Dutch is taking the day off, lucky thing."

This time the murmurs went unchecked. The duty mistress, her period of policing over, had taken her place among the other mistresses. As everybody rose from their seats at the entry of Miss Bulmer, the excited whispers, by no means lost in the shuffle of feet, continued. Miss Bulmer, grave-faced, walked slowly to the head's rostrum. She spoke no word; made no attempt to quieten the assembly. She stood and faced them, row upon row of youthful faces, and there was something in her attitude which brought them to silence. The whispering died, to be followed by a long moment of completely unbroken quiet. Only then did Miss Bulmer speak.

"Miss Holland," she said quietly and sadly, "died during the night."

It was a bombshell. All the brightness and happiness seemed to fade from the young faces as though some force had miraculously and slowly—as the realisation sank into their minds—removed masks of joy and replaced them with masks of sadness.

"I can tell you no more. Instead, however, of singing the hymn we were to have sung today, we will sing Mabel Holland's favourite hymn: 'Jerusalem the Golden'."

It was a subdued rendering, quiet and poignant. Miss Bulmer had chosen a special piece from the Scriptures—"And I saw a new Heaven and a new Earth"—and a suitable prayer. Her quiet words told. When she ended with the Grace, none of the movement which usually signalled the end of the little service took place.

"There will be no further games this week. Lessons will continue in the quiet and orderly manner as usual. Other mistresses will be along to take any periods normally taken by Miss Holland. Break will be taken out of doors. There will be no curb on conversation, but please behave quietly and sensibly. Everybody will leave the school premises promptly at four-thirty. That means any music or play rehearsals normally held between four thirty-five and five o'clock will be cancelled, and the fiction library will not open at that time. That is all."

The members of staff trooped solemnly off the stage. They had heard the news earlier, but had given nothing away before Miss Bulmer's announcement to the school. It would have been difficult to tell from their faces their inner thoughts about the sudden death of their head.

"Three A," said Miss Bulmer.

The row of side doors was opened by the prefects and the Upper Third, dismissed first, filed silently out of the hall.

One by one forms left when nominated. The prefects made their way to the back, where the school captain was collecting their absence reports, each written on a little sheet of paper from specially printed note pads. Form designation, date, absentees and (a section rarely, if ever, used) latecomers. The school captain, eighteen-year-old Melissa Craig-Deller, walked up the hall, as she did every morning, to hand the little forms to Miss Bulmer.

"Thank you, Melissa."

"Some of the younger girls were crying, Miss Bulmer."

"And some of the not so young, Melissa." Miss Bulmer glanced absent-mindedly at the papers in her hand. "You were at the back and so did not see their faces. From here I could detect a sense of shock. A definite sense of shock on two or three faces."

"I told the prefects that we would collect for a wreath, Miss Bulmer. They would like to do so, so that the flowers can go from the girls. We can do it quite quickly."

The deputy headmistress pursed her lips slightly. "Don't be in too much of a hurry, Melissa. There may be some delay."

The head girl stared for a moment. "Is there . . . is there something wrong, Miss Bulmer?"

"Not wrong, exactly, Melissa. But Miss Holland died unexpectedly, when she was apparently in the best of health. When that happens—when the person who dies hasn't received attention from a doctor for a long time—there has to be an inquest. That is the law, Melissa. A doctor has to certify the cause of death, and in Miss Holland's case, as she hadn't called on her doctor for more than two years, naturally he could not supply the certificate. So it could be that the formalities will take a little longer than they would normally. That is all. A short delay."

"I see, Miss Bulmer."

"You had better get along to first period now, Melissa. But, please, don't talk to your friends about what I just told you. It might start all manner of speculation about Miss Holland's death when, for all we know, it could have been, for instance, a simple heart attack or thrombosis."

"I'll say nothing, Miss Bulmer."

"Thank you, Melissa."

* * *

"Accident," said D.I. Lovegrove as he made his report to Chief Superintendent Hildidge, head of the Bramthorpe police. "Accident." He yawned as if to emphasise that he had been up all night and that the sudden death of the headmistress of a girl's school was more of a boring nuisance than anything else.

"Accident? What did she die of?"

"We don't know that yet, sir. But it was obvious she was poisoned. Her own doctor said so and the police surgeon. All the hallmarks of poison."

"You don't know what killed her, but you know it was an accident?"

"Either that or suicide, sir. God, I'm shagged. I could sleep for a week."

"Perhaps you would be kind enough—before you start snoring in that chair—to tell me why you are so certain it was accident, with the faint possibility that it might just be suicide?"

Something in Hildidge's voice should have warned the Detective Inspector that the Chief Superintendent was not too happy with so bald a report and so hasty a conclusion. But the nuance didn't register. Lovegrove yawned again, leaned further back in his superior's guest chair, crossed his feet and put his hands into his trouser pockets.

"Stands to reason, sir. This Holland dame . . ."

"Just one moment. I know we are told a prophet is not without honour save in his own country, Lovegrove. But I think I should remind you that Bramthorpe is one of the best and most highly thought of schools for girls in this country, and consequently in the world, and that Miss Holland is—or was—a headmistress without equal in the eyes of many people who know and care about these things. So less of the bit about this Holland dame."

"Sorry sir. I was forgetting your daughter went there. Must be costing you a packet. It would come cheaper at one of the local comprehensives."

"Hardly."

"No? I thought . . ."

"Never mind what you think, Lovegrove. For the record, my daughter, Helen, won one of the Bramthorpe Foundation Scholarships. She is getting a first-class education at a real comprehensive school for little more than it would cost me at one of the local schools. That being so, Lovegrove, you will realise that I am not only interested in Miss Holland's death, I am deeply and personally affected by it. So your report had better be made with those facts in mind. Now get on with it and make it good."

Lovegrove hauled himself, clumsily, into a more vertical position. He hadn't any idea why Hildidge was getting uptight about a sudden death. They were happening all the time. What did it matter, basically, how this headmistress had died? She was dead, wasn't she? Accident or suicide? It was immaterial. Just so long as there was no hint of foul play—which there wasn't—to interest the police professionally. But the Old Man sounded snarly. Was it the death of Miss Holland or had his missus bawled him out or burnt the breakfast toast? Whatever the cause, Lovegrove prudently decided to make a formal, verbal report; and that—barring the discovery and naming of the poison involved—would be that. He could then wrap the whole thing up with a written report in less than an hour.

"Miss Holland lives in the School House, sir."

"I know that, dammit."

"With a housekeeper, Mrs Gibson. She's the widow

of the man who was parks superintendent with Bramthorpe Council. She's a very respectable woman."

Hildidge nodded. Whether to imply he knew Mrs
Gibson's identity or to agree that she was a worthy
citizen was not apparent, but at least it encouraged
Lovegrove.

"She had yesterday off."

"Tuesday? That's a funny day to have off."

"That's what I said to her, but she reckons if she has
Wednesday off, it's half-day closing and she can't do
her bits of personal shopping unless she does them in
her boss's time."

"Get on with it."

"Mrs Gibson still has her old man's Mini. She uses
it for going to see her married daughters and her
grandchildren. She went off yesterday at ten in the
morning. Up to Petworth. Miss Holland was in school
till lunchtime. Then she had the afternoon to do
whatever headmistresses do in the afternoons in
schools where the kids play games every day."

Hildidge growled. "You don't know what you're
talking about, Lovegrove. Those girls work longer
hours than you do, most of the time. Games on Tuesday and Thursday afternoons. School matches Saturday afternoons. They're in school Monday, Wednes-
day and Friday afternoons, until half-past four—none
of your finishing at half-past three like most kids
round here—and they go to school on Saturday mornings until half-past twelve. Just to top it off, they do
two and a quarter hours of prep every night, and that
includes Saturdays. Work that out and you'll find it
comes to well over forty hours a week without their
games periods."

"Is that right, sir? I mean, the unions wouldn't wear
it."

14

"Of course it's right. That's why the place has its academic reputation."

"I see. Well, sir, Miss Holland returned to the School House for lunch, which used to be nothing more than biscuits and cheese, fruit and a cup of coffee. She used to get it for herself on Tuesdays, so presumably that's what she had. Then later in the afternoon she must have gone to Fellows the chemist's, to buy a few bits and pieces . . ."

Hildidge sat up. "What, exactly?"

"They were still there in the bag with the pay slip. Just some hand lotion and face powder and a couple of films. All accounted for on the bill."

"Have you seen the chemist?"

"Not yet, sir. He'll hardly be open yet."

"Go on."

"Mrs Gibson said Miss Holland was quite used to getting her own supper on Tuesdays if she wasn't going out to dinner, which she wasn't due to do last night. So Mrs Gibson had gone to the butcher before she went off yesterday morning and bought a bit of frying steak and some mushrooms . . ."

"Ah! Mushrooms! They could be the poison—if a toadstool had got in among them."

"That's what I thought, sir. But we'll have to wait and see what Forensic has to say."

"All right. What next?"

"Mrs Gibson got back at about half-past eleven. She let herself in the front door—it's an old mortise lock and she's got her own key—and she said she knew straight away there was something wrong."

"How?"

"She said there was a smell in the hall. Vomit. There was a light on on the stairs, and in the sitting

15

room. She looked in the room. The telly was still on, but Miss Holland wasn't about. So Mrs Gibson went to look for her. Half-way up the stairs was a great splodge of vomit. Then she got really worried."

"Why?"

"She reckoned Miss Holland was so meticulous that if she had puked on the stairs and it had made her feel better—like getting it up often does—she'd have cleaned up the mess. As she hadn't, she must still be pretty ill."

"Reasonable enough."

"Anyhow, she found Miss Holland lying on her own bed. She'd vomited to glory and the bedclothes were all scrunched up. She reckoned as soon as she saw her she knew she was dead. So she went downstairs and called the doctor. He arrived about midnight. He looked round for any bottles of stuff she could have taken, but there was nothing he could see, and then he called the nick. I got over there by about one o'clock. We searched the place. There wasn't anything —no drugs except a little slide pack of paracetamol and only three of those had been used, a half-empty bottle of cough linctus and some throat pastilles. And we examined the premises. No sign of any break-in and everything locked up tight. She was taken away for post mortem and the medics scraped up the puke for examination. They'll let us have their report by lunchtime with a bit of luck. And that's it, sir. She was alone in the house. Nobody broke in. As far as we know, nobody called. There's no toxic substance in the house."

"But she died of poison?"

"The medics say so. I can't argue with them. But what it was and how she came to get it, heaven only knows. It must have been an accident, sir, or, as I said, suicide, with nobody else implicated."

"So you say," grunted Hildidge, "but I met Miss Holland on a number of occasions. I'd have bet any money that she was not a woman to make a fatal mistake, which accident presupposes, and I'm damn sure she wouldn't commit suicide."

"We'll have to wait and see, sir."

"Wait? What for?"

"The forensic report, sir."

"And the inquest, I suppose?"

Lovegrove grimaced. "The coroner's verdict will tell us whether the case is closed or not."

"And with what you have to tell him, he'll give the same verdict as you."

"Why not? You know old Gilchrist. He doesn't like postponements. He likes a verdict immediately. He won't want to hang on *sine die* for us to make inquiries into what he thinks is an open-and-shut case. And that's how it should be. Over and done with. Tidier."

Hildidge looked across at the detective inspector with a certain amount of distaste. But he knew his subordinate was correct. Dr. Gilchrist was an autocratic coroner who gave the impression that he always knew best. He didn't like waffle. If the police could prove there was a case to investigate, he would play along with them. But without hard fact to suggest Miss Holland had met her death as the result of foul play, he would bring in an accident or suicide verdict. And yet Hildidge wasn't happy about it.

"Get off home for a few hours," he said to Lovegrove. "Be back here after lunch for when the forensic report comes in."

"Right, sir. I could do with forty winks."

DOUGLAS CLARK

* * *

Soon after Lovegrove had left him, Hildidge left his office and, taking his car, drove to Fellows' shop. The chemist himself came to the counter.

"Are you Mr Fellows?"

"Yes."

"You probably don't know me. I'm Chief Superintendent Hildidge."

"I've seen you about, Mr Hildidge. What can I do for you?"

"Answer a few questions, I hope."

Fellows eyed him warily. "Something wrong?"

"No, no. Nothing to do with you, at any rate."

"That's a relief. Come round to the dispensary. It's more private in there."

"Thank you." Hildidge followed the chemist into the back shop. "I won't keep you long. The point is that Miss Holland died rather suddenly last night."

"The headmistress? Why, she was in the shop yesterday afternoon. Here, wait a minute, Chief Superintendent, how did she die?"

"Of some sort of poison. Quite what, we don't know yet."

"You're not suggesting she got something here, I hope."

"Not at all. I said so, Mr Fellows."

"Then what's all this about?"

Hildidge said gloomily: "I suppose you'd call it her state of mind. We've got to decide how she came to die. She was all alone in the house. So it might have been accident, or it could have been suicide."

Fellows shook his head. "Not suicide. Not Miss Holland. She would never help herself to an overdose."

18

"It definitely wasn't an overdose of any drug or sleeping pills. There weren't any in the house."

"That's what I'd have guessed. And besides, her attitude here in the shop yesterday—why, she was telling Miss Dunn—she's my assistant—how much she was looking forward to going on holiday at the weekend."

"Going on holiday?"

"Yes. To Malta. Next week is half term. Miss Holland said she was going up to London on Friday afternoon to see her mother and stay the night and then going out to the airport on Saturday to fly to Malta. Said she was looking forward to getting the autumn sunshine out there. Reckoned it was the best time of the year to go. She was just buying a few cosmetics and a couple of films to take with her. In great fettle she was."

"You heard all this?"

"Yes. I was standing here in the doorway. We were quiet at the time. Miss Dunn and Miss Holland were only a few feet away, along the counter. I'd have said Miss Holland was the last person to commit suicide, without hearing her yesterday. But if ever I saw a well-balanced, happy woman, it was Miss Holland when she was chatting about her trip to Malta. I mean, it stands to reason, Mr Hildidge, nobody's going to do away with themselves when they've got a nice holiday coming up, are they?"

Hildidge grimaced thoughtfully. "It would seem you're right, Mr Fellows. I'll bear in mind what you've told me. And thanks. I don't suppose we'll have to worry you again, but it could just be we'll need a statement. If so, we'll have to have Miss Dunn confirm it, of course."

"Any time, Mr Hildidge. I'm only too thankful we

didn't sell her anything she could have taken a bit too much of by accident. I reckon her death is going to be a loss. We supply the school with all the bits and pieces for the matron and the first aid boxes and so on, and while Miss Holland's been there they've been ideal customers. I wish I had a hundred like them."

Hildidge took his leave of Fellows and made his way back to the station. As he passed the desk sergeant, he said: "I'll have a cup of black coffee sent up, please. And let me know when the forensic report on Miss Holland arrives."

"We've had a verbal, sir. The pathologist rang through to say she died of . . . Half a sec, sir, I've got it written down. Here it is. Miss Holland died of respiratory paralysis leading to death by asphyxia consequent upon the ingestion of cytisine. I was asked to tell Mr Lovegrove that cytisine is the poison in laburnum and it looks as if Miss Holland was chock full of the seeds."

"He said chock full?"

"Yes, sir. I took it down. There'll be a written report by tomorrow."

"Thanks. Anything else?"

"Yes, sir. Time of death between ten and eleven last night, sir. Not prepared to go any nearer than that."

"Right. Type up those notes and let me have a copy. And don't forget that coffee."

"Sir."

Hildidge worked in his office until well after midday. Fortunately it was mostly routine, because his mind was never entirely free of the business of Miss Holland's death. His concern was not solely on account of his own daughter, Helen, though he was of the opinion—maybe erroneous—that Bramthorpe would never again be the same school, and this could mean that Helen's education and upbringing would be the poorer. He was worried about the case. He had already satisfied himself that Lovegrove's hint of suicide was a non-starter. He'd known it wasn't suicide even before he had heard what Fellows had had to say. But equally he was sure accident could not be the answer. He had admired Miss Holland, and after long years in the police there were very few people he did admire. Admired and respected her because she had been—in his eyes—the essence, not of infallibility exactly, but of superb, practical intelligence of the sort that may make an error of judgement, always for the best of reasons, but that rarely makes mistakes. Certainly not major ones. And for her death to be an accident she would have needed to make the biggest mistake possible—a fatal one. And he just could not accept this, despite the fact that Lovegrove's investigations showed that no other party had been involved. The nagging problem was what to do about it. How to prove that his own feelings were right.

He tossed the last of the files into the out-tray, and as he did so, his internal phone rang.

The desk sergeant.

"Mr Hildidge, sir! Sir Thomas Kenny is here and would like to see you."

"I'll come down."

Sir Thomas Kenny was Chairman of the Bramthorpe Watch Committee and so was, in some respects, Hildidge's boss. But the Chief Superintendent guessed that Sir Thomas would be wearing another hat today. That of Chairman of the Board of Governors of Bramthorpe College, in which guise he had been Miss Holland's boss. The news of her death would have come as a great blow to Sir Thomas who—as Hildidge knew

21

—had as great a regard for the late headmistress as he had himself.

Hildidge went slowly downstairs. The prospects of interviewing the man who was, theoretically, responsible for ensuring that Bramthorpe was efficiently policed did not thrill him. He knew that he could offer Sir Thomas no report that would cover the force in glory or even offer a hint that the mystery was about to be cleared up.

"Good morning, Sir Thomas. This is a surprise. I'm sure I heard you were away on holiday."

"I am, or was. I hurried back as soon as I got the sad news about Miss Holland. My solicitor rang me as soon as he knew. I came straight back."

"You would like to discuss it with me?"

"That's why I'm here, Mr Hildidge."

They went up the stairs side by side. Compared with the Chief Superintendent, Kenny was small. A little, slim man, sixtyish, but still lithe, dressed in an expensive dark-grey suit, white silk shirt and black tie. He carried a dark, wide-brimmed hat of the style he customarily wore and which always gave Hildidge the impression that the little man had recently returned from some hot climate where it was necessary to shade eyes and face from the heat of the sun.

Kenny was a widower and—reputedly—a very rich man. He was certainly wealthy, owning businesses and a great deal of property in Bramthorpe. He had started in a small way and, by hard work and the unceasing use of an astute business mind, had climbed the ladder of financial success rapidly and skilfully.

"Can I offer you any refreshment, Sir Thomas? I have whisky or, if you prefer it, coffee."

"No, thank you." Kenny took the visitors' chair. "But I should like to hear what progress you have made in solving the mystery of Miss Holland's death."

Hildidge shrugged. "We have established that Miss Holland died from the poison which comes from laburnum seeds."

"Is that all?"

"We can find no evidence to show that anybody else was involved. She was alone in the house. There are no signs of forcible entry. All doors and windows were secure."

"You are saying she committed suicide?"

"No, sir. I personally believe that to have been impossible with Miss Holland. I know better than most that nobody can be sure of who will or who will not commit suicide, but if ever I was convinced of anything—knowing Miss Holland—it is that she would not take her own life. Also, we have evidence to show that she was in a very cheerful frame of mind yesterday and looking forward to a mid-term holiday in Malta."

Kenny nodded. "She was looking forward to it very much indeed, particularly as she had stayed in Bramthorpe and worked over most of the summer holiday." He looked up at Hildidge. "So what is your explanation, Mr Hildidge?"

"Laburnum poisoning is not uncommon, Sir Thomas. Many people die accidentally—particularly children—from picking up and chewing laburnum seeds in mistake for peas."

"You are saying this was an accidental death?"

"Up to now, sir, we can come to no other conclusion. My C.I.D. officers are still investigating, of course, but they are already convinced it was an accident."

"Can you envisage Miss Holland wandering about some garden and picking up seeds to chew, Hildidge?"

"No, sir."

"Yet you are treating her death as an accident."

23

There was no mistaking the almost scornful incredulity in Kenny's voice.

"Without firm evidence to the contrary, Sir Thomas, we have no option but to treat it as an accident or suicide. And our experience leads us to believe it will be one or the other. As we have ruled out suicide, we feel we are right in suggesting accidental death."

"Not this time." Kenny was adamant. He stared Hildidge straight in the eyes to emphasise his point.

Hildidge stared back for a moment. The little man was in deadly earnest and because the little man was also important, the Chief Superintendent was only too well aware that he had to treat what he was saying with extreme care.

"Sir Thomas," he said at last, "I have spent this morning wondering how Miss Holland came to die. I knew her—perhaps not as well as you, but as the parent of a pupil—and I must confess that not only am I at a loss to account for her death, but also that I am feeling her death, personally, very keenly. She was a woman I admired and respected, and in whose hands I was very glad to leave the education of my only daughter whom I prize above rubies. Do you not think, therefore, that I am as anxious as you to know how it happened and why?"

There was a silence. Then Hildidge continued.

"You are convinced her death was not accidental."

"Only accidental if it was an accident on somebody else's part, not on hers."

"You sound so positive, Sir Thomas, that I must ask you if you have some information for us. Perhaps that is why you hurried back from your holidays—to tell us something you think we ought to know."

"There is something I want to tell you, and it's

this. Miss Holland was no fool. She couldn't have poisoned herself with laburnum seeds accidentally."

"You don't necessarily have to be a fool to poison yourself accidentally, Sir Thomas."

"A biologist and botanist has to be."

"Miss Holland was a botanist?"

"Among other things."

"I didn't know that, Sir Thomas."

"And your people didn't bother to find out?"

"It had escaped our notice. We only learned this morning that the toxic substance was laburnum seeds. But now you've told us . . ."

"What will you do?"

"Sir Thomas, we can only work on facts."

"You mean you will still say it was an accident?"

"Unless we can prove otherwise."

"Which you believe to be impossible?"

"What exactly are you suggesting, sir? That Miss Holland was murdered? Because if it was neither suicide nor accident . . ." Hildidge didn't finish. He was wondering how best to appease Kenny and—if it came to that—his own suspicion, both apparently intent on forcing him into undertaking a full-scale murder investigation without a shred of reason for doing so. He was managing to suppress the urge of his own private belief—just—by constantly reminding himself that private beliefs unsupported by fact are notoriously bad reasons for starting a police case of such a nature. The two men stared at each other: Kenny determined and Hildidge at a loss. It seemed that the first to break the silence could well explode. It was then that Hildidge did what he ought to have done at the outset, and that was to say to hell with humouring Sir Thomas, no matter how important he was, and to do what he, the head of the local police, wanted to do. It was a police matter, and . . . He knew what he wanted to do. Had known it all along. Why had he held off? He supposed it was because of Lovegrove. Lovegrove who just wouldn't know how to handle a case like this.

"Well?" demanded Sir Thomas as though he had guessed Hildidge had come to a decision.

"I propose to ask the Chief Constable's permission to call in Scotland Yard, Sir Thomas. He will, of course, want sound reasons for agreeing. I shall try to give him those reasons, but I am relying on you to back me up. Without your help I may not succeed."

"Scotland Yard! Just what's needed, Hildidge. What I hoped you'd say. Don't worry about the Chief Constable. The only possible objection he can have is the expense, and if that happens I'll pay the bill myself and recover the money by not inviting him to dinner for the next two years."

Hildidge was pleased to see the little man had cheered up. When he thought about it, he realised that he himself felt happier, too.

He picked up the phone and asked for an outside line.

CHAPTER II

It was nearly three o'clock when D.I. Lovegrove knocked on the door of Hildidge's office and blundered in without waiting for an invitation.

"I heard downstairs you've called in the Yard," he said angrily.

"They'll be arriving at about half-past four."

"They can't do anything I haven't done."

"They can try."

"It won't alter the facts. And if the coroner brings in suicide or accident the case will be closed."

"What are your worried about, Lovegrove? If you've done everything possible, there'll be nothing for them to turn up. So you'll be in the clear. But if somebody turns up something you've missed . . ."

"Not a chance. There's nothing to turn up."

"You're sure?"

"Positive. Not a whisper of suspicion of anything more than suicide, really, though we'll have to call it an accidental death."

Hildidge didn't reply. He realised he was beginning actively to dislike Lovegrove. Hitherto he had tolerated the D.I., who normally did his everyday work well enough, but who had never sparked any feeling of friendship in the Chief Superintendent. The silence lasted long enough to make Lovegrove feel uncomfortable. He spoke first. "Anyway, what can these Yard chaps do between now and eleven o'clock tomorrow morning?"

"Why eleven o'clock?"

"That's when the inquest's arranged for."

Hildidge felt anger mounting. "Who arranged it?"

"The Coroner—Gilchrist—himself."

"With you?"

"Of course with me. Who else?"

"And you didn't ask him to hold off until we could be ready?"

"We are ready. I told you. I've got it all. Besides, Gilchrist couldn't manage Friday and he won't sit on Saturday, so it had to be Thursday, unless he held it over till next week. When I told him it would be accident or suicide, he said he wanted to get it cleared up as soon as possible."

"You've overstepped the mark, Lovegrove."

"How?"

Hildidge gestured helplessly.

"Look here, sir, I always arrange the inquests with the coroner in cases of unexplained death. It's part of my job. We've found no evidence of foul play, and when I arranged it I didn't know you were calling in the Yard. So how have I overstepped the mark? And what are you going to do about it? Tell Gilchrist to cancel because you think it is a case of murder although there's no evidence to support your opinion? You can do that, sir, but you won't get very far. Not with Gilchrist. He works on facts, as you very well know."

"Have you finished?"

"No, sir. I haven't. Who is going to represent the police tomorrow? Me, with what I've got? The only bloke who's done any of the investigation? Or are you going to suggest some big bug from Scotland Yard gets up just to say the police have nothing to present because they haven't made an investigation?"

Hildidge spoke quietly. "It could just be that you are right, Lovegrove, so I'll not say now what I think about this whole set-up. But if it turns out you're wrong, then I'll have something to say both privately and officially. Now go and get some work done."

Lovegrove left the office and Hildidge sat back to think. The D.I. had been right. Gilchrist was not the sort of man to postpone an inquest, once arranged, without good reason. He would regard such a request as Hildidge could make as trivial and possibly as an attempt to trifle with his office. There was also the chance of exposing a rift in Hildidge's own force if the D.I. had told Gilchrist there was no evidence of foul play and he, Hildidge, were to suggest there could be but could produce no evidence to support the claim. He damned Lovegrove, and then himself for not having acted more positively and taken over the reins once it had been decided to call in the Yard. He supposed there was nothing he could do now except consult the Yard man when he arrived. They had said they were sending Masters—Detective Superintendent George Masters. He'd heard of him. Heard of his reputation as a Jack as good as any the Yard had produced for a long time. An ideas man, he'd been called. Hildidge hoped he would have some ideas about how Miss Holland came to meet her death.

It was just after half-past four when Masters, together with Detective Chief Inspector Green and Detective Sergeants Reed and Berger were shown into Hildidge's office by a visibly overawed desk sergeant.

"Sit down," urged Hildidge, after the introductions

were over. "I've arranged accommodation for you, but I'd very much like to talk to you before you go off to settle in. I'll have some tea sent up."

When they were all sitting with tea and biscuits, Hildidge said: "I'll be honest with you. We've found no reason to suppose Miss Holland was murdered. What we're going on is a conviction that it could not be suicide, that she was not the woman to take a huge dose of poison seeds by mistake, her really outstanding character, and the same opinions expressed very forcibly by Sir Thomas Kenny who is chairman of our Watch Committee and also Chairman of the Governors of the school."

"Local big-wig, is he?" asked Green, his mouth full of custard cream.

"Actually," said Hildidge with a smile, "he's a little chap. No more than three teacups and a chamber-pot high."

Green obviously liked the description. "The Great I-Am, then?"

"Something of the sort. But I can understand his interest in the case. I knew Miss Holland, because my daughter is at the school. But Sir Thomas tells me the Governors are of the opinion that in Miss Holland they had one of the best, if not the best, in the headmistress line. She'd been at the school just over three years and had gilded the lily. Improved on excellence was how Sir Thomas put it."

"What has been done so far?" asked Masters.

Hildidge spent the next ten minutes describing the events of the previous night and what Lovegrove had done. When he paused, Green said: "That's the lot, is it?"

"I'll give you the file, of course. Not that there's anything in it. Lovegrove has it at the moment. He'll

30

have it ready for you—with the forensic report, I hope
—tomorrow morning."

"When is the inquest?" asked Masters.

"Tomorrow morning at eleven, in the courtroom at
the town hall."

"You realise that if there is no evidence of murder
by then the coroner's verdict could close the case before it has started?"

"I do. And I'm sorry about it." Hildidge explained
the circumstances and spoke of Gilchrist's autocratic
handling of his court.

"It appears we may be scuppered either way," said
Masters. "Without evidence of foul play, Gilchrist
will bring in his verdict based on what Lovegrove can
tell him. And he won't hold over, either, without
evidence to support his decision?"

"I think not. It would be out of character were he to
do so."

"I see," Masters looked at Hildidge. "We'll have to
think about it tonight and see what we can do. Meanwhile, there was one point that interested me. You
said Miss Holland intended to visit her mother on
Friday night."

"Yes."

"Do you happen to know why?"

Hildidge shook his head. "Is it important?"

"You led us to believe Miss Holland did few things
without a purpose. To go to London on Friday night,
merely to travel out to Heathrow on Saturday, would
seem to be a pointless exercise as she could get to
Heathrow much more easily from here."

"So?"

"I'm wondering whether there was some specific
reason for the more difficult journey. Has her mother
been told of her death?"

"We phoned through early this morning to the nearest police station and got them to take the news round."

"Has her mother been told of the inquest?"

"Lovegrove is certain to have informed her."

Masters turned to Green. "Bill, would you find out if Mrs Holland is on the phone at home? If so, get in touch and ask her if she knows why her daughter intended to visit her on Friday night. It might only have been intended as a sort of duty call, but there could be something else, and if there is, we ought to know about it."

Green shrugged. "We've got to fish around somewhere if we've only got until eleven tomorrow morning." He got up and left the office.

Matsers turned back to Hildidge. "I would prefer not to work contrary to the coroner's verdict. If we could persuade him to open and then postpone . . . that is what we must attempt to do, in open court."

"I wish you luck. Gilchrist really has a strong objection to being approached by the police. I reckon he regards it as subversion of justice."

Masters filled his pipe with Warlock Flake. Reed asked Hildidge: "Sir, am I right in thinking that your D.I. has gone solid on suicide or accident? Or is he backing you and Sir Thomas Kenny?"

"That's a hard question to answer, Sergeant."

"Meaning he thinks we're going to get nothing."

"What would you think in his place?"

"I'd be beavering away to wipe the Yard's eye."

"Then you have your answer."

Before Reed could go further, Green returned. He walked across the office and sat down before speaking. Then he said: "You've hit the nail on the head, George. Miss Holland sometimes rang her mum, but she was a great believer in reviving the lost art of letter-writing."

Masters nodded and applied a match to his pipe.

"Mrs Holland got a letter on Tuesday morning—yesterday—telling her that Mabel would be visiting her on Friday night."

"Any particular reason?"

"Oh, yes."

"What?"

"Not specified." Green took a slip of paper from his pocket. "I took down the gist of it. Mrs Holland said that according to the letter, Mabel said she was very happy and excited, that something wonderful had happened and that she, Mabel, knew her mum would be overjoyed by the news, so she was saving it up as a lovely surprise for her on Friday night."

"Not even a hint as to what it was?"

"Nothing at all. But does it matter?"

"Not in the least as long as we get the letter."

"I told her to bring it with her. Told her it was very important and that one of the sergeants would meet her train at the station."

"Good." Masters got to his feet. "If we could have a guide to our hotel, Mr Hildidge . . .?"

The big Rover followed the Panda car to the Planet, which from the outside showed itself to be a modern, medium-sized hotel, all concrete and glass, with a car park in front.

"Three-star," said Reed. "Shouldn't be bad."

It was Masters who went to the reception desk. It was while he was giving details of his party that Green said in a loud whisper: "Not bad, you said, lad. See where we've landed ourselves?"

Masters turned to see what was going on. Green

said, with something approaching horror in his voice: "They've put us in a temperance pub, George."

"That's a contradiction in terms."

"Maybe. But read this." Green thrust a brochure into Masters' hand. The Superintendent read the information pointed out to him on the back of the cover.

> The Planet Hotel is unlicensed. Wines, Spirits and Beers, in sealed bottles, may be obtained on behalf of Guests by the Head Waiter for ready cash at the time of ordering. Alternatively, Guests may introduce their own supplies, on which no corkage will be charged.

"I knew there'd be something wrong with this Bramthorpe dump," grumbled Green. "No case to investigate without we invent our own, and a temperance hotel. As my old mother-in-law used to say, 'What I've lived to see!' "

"Wait, wait," urged Masters. "You can bring in any drink you like at retail prices. They'll be a damn sight cheaper than bar prices."

"I like somewhere to lean my elbows."

"Maybe, but we'll make do. We've no time to run around looking for a different place. Everybody sign in, and then we'll have a word. I'll be in 211. Reed, how about bringing in a couple of dozen bottles of Ruddles before you join us? Take the car and find an off-licence."

Reed nodded, and Masters, not waiting for the lift, took his room key and luggage and set off up the stairs.

"Reed not back yet?" asked Green.

"Not yet. But come in. What's your room like?"

"Same as this. They're all built to the same pattern. Twin beds and internal bathroom. Quite comfy, really."

Berger joined them. As they sat waiting for the beer Berger said: "Chief, I don't understand all this rush to present some sort of case by tomorrow morning. I always thought there was nothing to prevent the police carrying on an investigation whatever the coroner's verdict."

Green said: "So we can, in theory, lad. But there are arguments against it, particularly in this case."

"What arguments?"

There was a heavy knock at the door. "This'll be Reed with the beer. I'll let him in while His Nibs answers your question."

Reed had brought glasses up with him from the dining room. He and Green opened the squat bottles of Ruddles while Masters explained to Berger the reason why he was so anxious to find at least a little hint of a suggestion of foul play by the time the inquest had started.

"If the locals were to do their own investigating, they could go ahead regardless. But investigations which include the presence of a team such as ours cost money and time. Most people would say there can be little justification for continuing a case which a coroner has satisfied himself is suicide or accidental death and in which neither the local police nor ourselves can produce a single shred of fact to say he is wrong. Mr Hildidge has called us in because he himself and Sir Thomas Kenny—neither of whom is exactly impartial in his assessment of the woman's character—think that Miss Holland was not the type to commit suicide or make a fatal mistake. You don't need me to point out the flaws in their belief. They really are not grounds for calling us in to begin with, so what justification can there be for keeping us here on such a flimsy pretext in the face of a coroner's unfavourable verdict? He'd have to send us packing. If, however, we could somehow persuade the coroner of the need to bring in an open verdict or to adjourn, then at least we should have some excuse—a duty, in fact—to investigate exhaustively to the point where we should eventually be able to satisfy the coroner or, if necessary, a criminal court. Unfortunately, the local coroner —according to Hildidge, who should know—will only proceed or pronounce on fact. Therefore, tomorrow morning, fact there must be, or we are out of a job."

Green handed Berger a glass. "What His Nibs is saying, lad, is that if we don't look slippy we've had it. And don't think he's maximising our difficulties. He isn't."

"But that letter . . ."

"Could help—just."

"I see."

"Not bad stuff this," said Green, holding his glass up to the light. "Nice and amber, but above all, clear. I wish the case was."

"Let's try to clarify it," said Masters, sitting on one of the beds because Green had occupied the armchair. "We are agreed that we've got to get over the big hurdle of tomorrow's inquest before we can start to investigate properly. Normally, we have little to do with inquests, leaving them to the locals to sort out. But I have a nasty feeling about this one. Hildidge called us in to satisfy himself and Kenny. But what about Lovegrove? I got the impression that he would like to take the first excuse he can grab to lever us out."

"Hildidge said as much, Chief."

"True. He didn't actually put it in so many words because he didn't want to be disloyal to one of his own subordinates. But remember that the mere fact of inviting us here must have been a blow to Lovegrove—an indication that Hildidge doesn't trust him to handle the case. So Lovegrove, I believe, will reckon that the lever he wants to get us out will be tomorrow's verdict. All that business about the reluctance of the coroner to play along with the police is playing straight into Lovegrove's hands."

"How come, Chief? Exactly, I mean?"

"Lovegrove will be appearing for the locals. He's got to, because he's the investigating officer. But he's not going to ask for an adjournment or an open verdict. He'll suggest—regretfully—that he has no evidence on which to base such a request, and he'll take damn good care his evidence doesn't give the coroner cause even to contemplate murder."

"That's unless we turn something up between now and then, you mean, Chief?"

"Quite."

"Are we likely to?"

"The odds are against it. And even if we were to do so, I don't think I'd like Lovegrove to present it."

"You could do it yourself."

"No coroner would accept two officers to represent the police—with conflicting evidence, that is. He'd want to know why there was a lack of co-ordination."

Green sucked his partial denture. "You got any ideas, George?"

"Talk it through with me."

"Brainstorm?"

"If you like. Lovegrove, tomorrow, will present evidence, the burden of which will be that there is no cause to suppose Miss Holland's death was anything

37

other than suicide or accident. He will certainly produce no fact to suggest murder."

"Chief," said Reed. "There's just one thing."

"What's that?"

"It could be that Lovegrove hasn't produced anything to suggest murder because it isn't murder."

"I'll accept that. I'll also accept that we have only the flimsiest grounds for initiating a murder inquiry in view of a nil return—as it were—from Lovegrove."

"But?" grinned Reed.

"But I query the nil return. What I mean is, did Lovegrove ever seriously consider murder? From the fact that Hildidge says the file is empty, and from what Hildidge himself told us of the steps Lovegrove had taken—or hadn't taken, if you think of Fellows the chemist and the letter to Mrs Holland, neither of which he discovered—I judge that Lovegrove did not consider the possibility of murder, and if he didn't, he didn't look. And if he didn't look, he didn't unearth the facts. So the nil return was inevitable."

"And the same applies," said Green, "even if he did start to look. What I mean is, if it occurred to Lovegrove that this could be murder, but then, because he found Miss Holland alone and uninjured, with the house locked up and no sign of entry, he would dismiss the idea of foul play without looking further."

"Quite so," agreed Masters. "Don't forget they discovered she had been to the chemist yesterday afternoon and accepted that as the last time she was seen alive. This led them to suppose that she had returned home by, say, four o'clock for a cup of tea. So—they will argue—she was probably alone for nearly seven hours before she died, by the forensic reckoning. But cytisine—certainly in the large dose she is reported as having taken—does its work in far less time than that.

Say three to four hours. So Lovegrove will argue she was alone for seven hours and perfectly well for the first half of that time. The easy conclusion is suicide —or accidental death."

"And to counter that," growled Green, "we only have character references from Hildidge, old Sir Tosh, and Ma Holland's letter."

"Right. And don't forget we can't call Hildidge and Kenny to say what they think. That wouldn't be evidence."

"Huh!" grunted Green. "Let's have some more of that beer, young Berger."

"So doing something before eleven tomorrow morning, Chief, is impossible, barring miracles," said Reed.

Masters nodded and then said slowly: "There may be an alternative."

"What?" asked Green.

"If we can't do anything *before* eleven tomorrow morning, we must be prepared to do something *at* eleven tomorrow morning. Or shortly after."

Green stopped half-way through pouring another glass of beer and stared at Masters. "What are you suggesting? That we should kidnap Lovegrove?"

"Hardly. I meant I would ask to take the stand at the inquest."

"You can't. Lovegrove will never yield to you and, in any case, you haven't started your investigation yet, so you can't appear."

"Yes, I can," asserted Masters. "As a private citizen. The Crowner's Quest is an ancient British institution set up to inquire into whatever is set before it, and though it is formalised these days into the Coroner's Inquest, it is still the duty of all citizens who have knowledge or information concerning the subject of the inquiry to present themselves and say their piece."

"Fair enough," said Green, "but the coroner will still want facts, and he won't let you speak unless you've got facts to present. Relevant facts."

Masters got to his feet and moved to the window. For a moment or two he stood looking out over the concrete outbuildings at the back of the hotel. Nobody spoke. At last he turned and said: "I think we have got some facts. Not very good ones, perhaps, but they're all we've got so I'll have to use them. Quite frankly, I'm counting on pulling rank. . . ."

"As a private citizen, Chief?" asked Berger sceptically.

"It could work," said Green. "His Nibs appears as a private citizen, but it doesn't alter the fact that he's still a Detective Superintendent from the Yard. No coroner is going to ignore that and bring in a verdict of suicide or accident when he knows a senior Yard officer has other ideas." He wagged a finger at Berger. "It stands to reason, lad. Put yourself in the coroner's place. Would you bring in a verdict of suicide knowing that inside a week a bloke like His Nibs could prove you wrong?"

"Particularly when there are two nice, easy ways open to you," added Reed. "An open verdict or an adjournment."

"I suppose I wouldn't," replied Berger, answering Green's question. "Not after a warning by the Chief. But I know him. Gilchrist doesn't. And what are the facts he is going to produce?"

Masters held his glass out for more beer. "I shall have to work up what we've got," he said. "But the main thing is, Sergeant, that I believe in what I'm doing, otherwise I wouldn't do it."

"You think she was murdered?"

"I didn't say that. I believe we should be given the

40

chance to inquire: that investigation should not be stifled."

"I see."

"You know I steer clear of inquests: avoid them like I avoid fields with bulls in them. They're not my scene. I grow impatient with them. Wrongly, perhaps, because they have a useful function. But that's beside the point. It's a question of confidence in our cause and I hope that that is what will come through in whatever I have to say at the inquest, and that it will help to sway the coroner as much as the cachet of my rank."

"Good points, all of them," agreed Green. "And there's something else we might be able to count on. Hildidge said Gilchrist is an autocratic old sinner. That means—ten to one—that he'll be strong for law and order. If you can hint that what you're asking for is the chance to uphold old-fashioned L and O, you'll get a sympathetic hearing, George."

"Let's hope so. Now the facts. As yet there is only one I can put forward as incontrovertible. And that is Miss Holland's great knowledge of botany. I can ram home the fact that she would never take laburnum seeds by mistake.

"The other things which might help are first, her intention to go on holiday, with the chemist's evidence of a stable, even happy, state of mind to back me up. Second, the letter to her mother talking about some piece of news so wonderful that properly to impart it she was intending to make an inconvenient and unnecessary journey to London.

"So I think I can argue that both accident and suicide would not be safe findings. And that, so far, is all I've got."

"We'll have to coach Fellows and Mrs Holland,"

said Green. "Get them to emphasise how happy, successful and about-to-go-on-holiday a woman she was."

"True. I'll leave that to you, Bill. And also to see Mrs Gibson, the housekeeper, to see if she can back the other two up. Certainly we don't want her to put a spoke in our wheel."

"Right. Leave her to me."

"Thanks. After dinner, then, you and Berger go to the School House and interview Mrs Gibson. Reed and I will try to see Sir Thomas Kenny at the same time."

"For any particular reason, Chief?"

"He was one of the prime movers in getting us here, so he may have facts to back up his feelings. But, in any case, I don't know who else to see at this stage, and we must try to get more ammunition for tomorrow."

"Right. Dinner now?"

"Two phone calls first. Bill, would you ring the School House and see if Mrs Gibson is there? She should be, as it's her home, and I can't think that she'll be out gadding about at a time like this. I'll look up Kenny's number and ask him to see me. After that, scoff."

Luck was with them. Both interviews were on. Masters and Reed would drop Green and Berger at the school and then go on to see Sir Thomas. Whoever finished the interview first would ring through to the other to arrange the pick-up.

It was dark by the time Green and Berger were dropped at the main door of the school on Sinclair Hill. After the Rover left them, they needed to spend a few minutes to get their bearings.

The main door was of oak, solidly built and double-leaved, with small panes of glass so heavy that they had to be chamfered at the edges to go into the mouldings which held them. It stood, under an arched porch of stone, at the top of a wide flight of eight steps bordered by iron balustrades. The building line of the school was thus only a few feet back from the pavement of the hill. On either side of the steps was a carefully built brick wall, tapering off to a mere three feet high at the top end and a forbidding seven feet at the lower end. Behind this wall they could see—by the light of the lamp standards on the pavement—that the ground had been levelled and the area between it and the front of the building planted with scores of bushes, some evergreen but most, Berger commented, selected to flower at different times of the four seasons.

"Where do we get in?" asked Berger.

"Not here, at any rate. I'll bet this is never opened except for parents and governors and such."

"There are gates at both ends of the wall."

They walked downhill. Here they came to a pair of large wrought-iron gates, tall, well-painted and carrying what Green rightly assumed to be the school crest picked out in colour.

"This is where the kids come in. That's the end of a bike shed up there." He looked along the side wall of the school building. "There's four doors there."

The light was not good enough to see details, but he had guessed correctly. The two middle doors of the four were the two leading directly into the cloakrooms. The more distant one was the staff door and gave directly onto the long, high corridor which ran the full length of the back of the school and off which, on the far side, opened the majority of the form rooms. The nearest of the four was different. This was a double door, through which could be carried any large item such as desks or pianos. And, though Green could not see it, it had a bell beneath which was a little brass plate bearing the word "Secretary".

The big gates were locked.

"We're not going to get in this way."

They turned and climbed the hill to the other gate. This was a normal double gate to admit a car, such as any house might have. To assure them that they had at last found what they wanted, a name plate which said simply "School House", was fastened to one of the pillars. They went through. The drive led past the end of the long front block of the school and there, tucked in round the corner, was the house. It looked— even in the dark—as though it had been built on as an afterthought to the secondary block which, like the one at the other end containing the four doors, linked the two large front and rear portions of the school.

"I've got it," said Berger. "This place is built like an H with an extra cross-bit across the bottom. The house is in the top bit, and there'll be a hole between the two bottom bits."

"That hole you speak of," said Green, "will as like as not be an enclosed quadrangle. Sort of hallowed ground with turf like velvet on which even the head groundsman will only be allowed to stand if he takes his boots off."

"Places like this have some daft traditions, don't they?"

"Daft? Maybe. But they get nice bits of grass because of them."

They passed through another little gate, and up a short path to the front door of the house. Berger pulled the bell.

Against the light in the hall, the woman who answered the door was plumpish and grey. Green put her down as a matronly sixty.

"Mrs Gibson?"

She ushered them in politely enough, but she seemed nervous, suspicious even. Green guessed she had had her fill of callers—police, reporters, sympathisers, busybodies.

"I'm the one who rang you."

"From Scotland Yard?"

"That's right. My name is Green, and this is Sergeant Berger. We'd like to talk to you."

"So you said. But I've been over it all once with that Lovegrove man."

"I know. But we've taken over. You'd like us to get to the bottom of things, wouldn't you?"

"I should just think I would. You come into my room, Mr Green." She led them into a comfortable little sitting room. "Sit down. You can move my knitting off that chair. . . ."

"Cosy here," said Berger, lifting the knitting on its needles and a long, rectangular tin which had once contained shortbread but which now, judging by the rattle of it, had been pressed into service as a sewing box.

"Miss Holland made sure I was comfortable. 'Three armchairs you need, Mrs Gibson,' was what she said. 'No chesterfields or sofas unless you start courting again and want room for two.' Always humorous, she was. Laughed at me, always knitting for my daughters' kiddies. I used to have a knitting bag until it wore out and I started to use that tin. My nutting bag, she called it, and always laughed when she said it."

"She was a cheerful soul, was she?" asked Green, choosing the chair directly opposite Mrs Gibson. "Right up to the end?"

45

"As happy as Larry," declared the housekeeper. "That's why I think it's about time you people arrived instead of those local men."

"You haven't much confidence in them?"

"The way they carried on?"

"What did they say, exactly?"

"First off, suicide. I told them they could think again, so they said accident. 'How could it be an accident?' I asked. Of course, we didn't know then what she'd died of. But they told me this afternoon. Laburnum seeds."

"And still said it was an accident?"

"Yes. But it couldn't be. There isn't a laburnum tree anywhere near this house. Or in the school grounds. Trees all round the playing field, I told them, but horse chestnuts and limes, mostly, with one oak and a few elms—all dead now and replanted with a few little saplings. I know what's round here. My husband was head groundsman here at one time—before he became parks superintendent—and as far as I know there isn't a laburnum anywhere near."

"What did the local police say to that?"

"Silly chumps, they were. 'She could have gone out and collected the seeds,' they said. 'Where from?' I asked. 'The headmistress of Bramthorpe going into somebody's garden and picking up seeds? That would be the day!' I said. 'And when?' I asked. 'Any time,' they said. 'Oh, yes?' I asked. 'And when are laburnum seeds ripe?' "

"That's a point," said Green. "When do they ripen?"

"There you are, you see! You don't know anything about them, either." She explained as to a child. "The flowers come—they're in yellow clusters, you know, called racemes—in May and June. Then you get the first pod with six or eight seeds in it. The seeds go dark brown when ripe and fall off."

"Just a moment," said Green. "Why are we talking about ripe seeds?"

"Because at this time of the year they couldn't be anything else. Hard, dry, dark brown. And it was little dark bits the doctors found inside her."

"I've not seen the forensic report yet, so I'll take your word for it. What did the locals say to what you told them?"

"Nothing. They thought she could have eaten them instead of peas. But I wish I hadn't said anything. I'd have been better to keep my own counsel, because then they went back to saying it was suicide if it couldn't be accident."

"What did you say to that?"

" 'Murder', I said, and they laughed."

"Why?"

"Because of what I'd told them about what happened yesterday."

"What did happen?"

"Nothing. That's just it. Miss Holland went into school as usual just before nine. As soon as she'd gone I did our bit of shopping. A bit of steak for her dinner—easy for her to cook for herself as I wasn't going to be here to do it for her."

"It was your day off?"

"Every Tuesday."

"Who decided on steak? Instead of a chop or a nice bit of gammon, say?"

"I did. I always get her steak because it's easy to do, and she was no great shakes as a cook."

"Fair enough. What else did you buy?"

"Some mushrooms, bananas, and a packet of starch—oh, and some sweets for my grandchildren. Then I came back, put the things away, had a cup of coffee and set off to see one of my daughters."

"Had Miss Holland told you what her programme for the day was? Did she say she was expecting anybody to call?"

"Nobody. She said so, at breakfast. She wouldn't be in school on Tuesday afternoon, so she said she was going to wash her smalls and go to the chemist for a few things she wanted for her holiday."

"She did her own washing?"

"Just her tights, pants and bras. I'd offered to do them often enough, but she reckoned any woman should do those for herself."

"I see. Please go on."

"After that she'd have some clerical work to do. There's always a lot of it, and as she was going on holiday she wanted to be sure it was all done before she went."

"She was a well-organised woman?"

"Like clockwork. At one o'clock she'd have her lunch. Only biscuits and cheese and fruit."

"Nothing else?"

"As it was Tuesday, she might have had a glass of sherry beforehand. Never on a full schoolday, though. She said it would make her too sleepy in the afternoon. And she'd have had a cup of coffee, too."

"After lunch she did her laundry and went to the chemist and then came back to work?"

"I think her smalls were probably dry by the time she got back. Anyhow, she ironed them. They're all in the airing cupboard."

"Would she have made herself a cup of tea?"

"Nothing surer. With lemon was how she liked it. Never missed."

"Even on full schooldays?"

"She only had three afternoons in school. Mondays, Wednesdays and Fridays, and she never taught in the last period. But even if she was staying in the school study I took a tray through there at a quarter to four."

"When did school end?" asked Berger.

"At half-past four."

"As late as that?"

"For the big girls. This is a proper school. Afternoon school starts at a quarter past two. Three periods of three quarters of an hour each, and no breaks in the afternoon either. Never any changes in timings, or timetable, and all teachers there on the dot. Stop one class at one minute before the bell and start the next one at one minute after. That is what Miss Holland laid down. Of course, she'd got it arranged so that there weren't many forms of girls moving about unnecessarily. It was the teachers that moved. Her timetables were worked out a lot better than D-day operations and, I daresay, worked a lot better, too."

Green said he was pleased to hear it, but he began to wonder whether such strict discipline—however kindly imposed—had not upset somebody in these days of no-discipline education. He kept the thought to himself, however, and asked: "After doing her ironing and having a cup of tea, then what?"

"I think it would have been five o'clock by then."

"Would that be important for some reason?"

"That's when she always did her marking."

Berger looked surprised. "When I was at school we were lucky if we got anything marked, and when we did, the teachers didn't do it in their own time. They did it in ours, or in all those free periods they spent drinking tea in the staff room."

"This is a proper school," reiterated Mrs Gibson, thereby consigning Berger's alma mater and all other comprehensives to—perhaps—just one rung above Borstal on the status ladder of educational establishments.

"My headmaster didn't teach classes. At least, not much." Berger said this defensively, as though not doing what he was paid to do was a point in favour of the gentleman mainly responsible for his education.

"We don't have classes here. Forms. Miss Holland taught the Upper Fifth and Sixth *forms*."

"So she would do her marking at five o'clock," said Green pacifically.

"And preparing the next day's lessons. Just for an hour. Then she'd go for her bath."

"At six?"

"She'd listen to the news."

"Listen? Not watch?"

"The television is in the sitting room. She had a radio in her house-study where she did her marking."

"So it would have been half-past six . . ."

"If she was going out, she only listened to the headlines."

"But she wasn't going out, yesterday?"

"She told me she wasn't."

"And she wasn't expecting anybody?"

"No. Not at the time I left, that is."

"Right. So she'd go and have a bath and come down again. . . . When?"

"On the stroke of seven, always."

"Why?" asked Berger. "Why was she always so precise?"

"Because it was the logical thing. She always said seven o'clock was right if she was going out, because everything in Bramthorpe starts at half-past. It was right if she was staying in, because we always had dinner at half-past, and I had to know when it would be

50

wanted. And if she had guests they were always invited for half-past seven."

Mrs Gibson obviously thought this explanation good enough for Berger, and turned to face Green. "We had this house going like clockwork, me and Miss Holland."

"So it seems. But, unfortunately, you weren't here to cook her supper last night."

"I'll never forgive myself for being away. Never. But not because of the cooking. I told you, I brought her in a nice bit of steak to grill. Wouldn't take her more than the shake of a lamb's tail to do it, being that tender. And she had it."

"How do you know?"

"Because it had gone from the fridge."

"She washed up after her?"

"Oh, yes. Grill pan as well."

"What else did she eat besides steak? Do you know?"

"Yes. A bit of deep custard. I made it on Monday."

"With nutmeg on top?"

"Smothered in it, just how she liked it. . . . Here, you're not saying . . .?"

"Not saying what, Mrs Gibson?"

"That my nutmeg wasn't nutmeg."

"Did the locals test it?"

"No, they didn't."

"Is there any of the custard left?"

"No. I ate it myself. The last bit tonight, in fact, and I'm still here."

"So it was nutmeg," said Berger. "But you must admit, little brown bits . . ."

"Nothing in my kitchen was poison."

"Something was, somewhere," said Green.

"Not in my kitchen."

51

"Let's get on. Miss Holland cooked her steak and had her supper. She'd be finished well before eight if she started to cook at seven, wouldn't she?"

"It all depends what she had with the steak."

"What did you leave her?"

"Everything. Onions, tomatoes, mushrooms, carrots, peas in the freezer, potatoes. . . ."

"Won't the forensic reports tell us?" asked Berger.

"Yes. But I can't see Miss Mabel Holland—the one that's been described to me, that is—after she'd had her bath, coming down and peeling onions. She'd have something easy like the mushrooms Mrs Gibson brought in or tomatoes. So cooking the meal would not take long, and when somebody is alone, it doesn't take long to eat, either. So I reckon she'd be through eating and washing up by eight. So what would she do then?"

"She'd read or watch telly," said Mrs Gibson. "Depending on what was on. She was particular what she watched."

"No pop or anything like that?"

Mrs Gibson pursed her lips. "Miss Holland did her job properly. Usually she watched documentaries and plays. But now and again she'd listen to a bit of pop because she thought she ought to."

"Oh? Why?"

"Because the girls all listen to it, don't they? And she thought she ought to try and understand or know something about it. She wouldn't allow transistors to be brought to school, of course. Very down on that, she was. But the boarders can have them in their houses —but only to play at certain times. Not after lights out or anything like that."

"Did any of the girls resent it?"

"How should I know? I don't know much about

52

what went on actually in the school. Only what I picked up in here."

"No details. Just Miss Holland's general attitude?"

"That's right. What she really needed was a family to talk to, but as she hadn't got one, she spoke to me, see. She was mostly a busy woman at nights—going here, there and everywhere on committees and speaking, as well as living her social life. But on Sundays, particularly, we were just here together. She always refused to work on Sundays, saying it was a day of rest and she reckoned she could do her job better if she really lazed about the house for one day a week. So after the morning service—she always went with the boarders—we gossiped a lot over elevenses and read the papers and such like. She never wanted me to cook big meals at weekends, so if she was in for the evening we always had a salad with bubble and squeak if we had any left-overs. She adored bubble and squeak. And that's when she used to tell me things. Little things. Nothing about anybody in particular, but it all added up, and I got to understand what she thought about everything."

"Such as?"

"Such as? Oh, well . . . the plans she had for getting school prizes out of people. The old prizes, she said, weren't good enough. She wanted the girl who won the essay prize to have fifty pounds' worth of books of her own choosing. She said the old five-pound prize wasn't big enough to attract first-class entries. And all that sort of thing. So, you see, I got to know her attitude about prizes, didn't I? A lot of schools, she said, want to do away with prizes for work and even stop exams. Miss Holland believed in having something to work for and to be encouraged by."

Green grunted—whether in approval or otherwise

was not apparent. "Now, Mrs G., she would have read or watched telly, you say, from about eight o'clock on. You're sure she wasn't expecting a caller?"

"She said definitely not, but somebody could have called, of course."

"Did they, sometimes?"

"Not often. Not at night."

"Let's try to see if they did."

"How can we do that?"

"If somebody came after dinner at night, what usually happened? Did Miss Holland offer them a drink or a cup of coffee?"

"Always."

"Did callers usually accept?"

"Never knew one that didn't. At that time of night you don't call in for two minutes or to leave a message, do you? You ring up for that. No, if anybody came, they'd have stayed for a bit, I'd have said. And they'd have had a drink, too."

"Right. What happened to the dirties after an evening drink?"

Mrs Gibson gazed at him. "You're right. They were always left on the draining board until morning. Miss Holland always said there was no point in wasting good hot water and soap to wash up a few dishes late at night. She always laughed when she said it, because it was only an excuse for not doing it. And that went for any cups and glasses we may have used, even when there wasn't a visitor."

"Fine. So Miss Holland, being a creature of habit . . ."

"Not habit exactly. Not in a finnicky way. She'd worked out the best way for doing habitual things and stuck to it. I think she was so busy that she was frightened that if she didn't have method, some things wouldn't get done. But she did do lots of things on the spur of the moment like everybody else. Her way of ordering her life was more like having a sort of skeleton for the day, just to keep things straight. But everything else was, you know . . . different and interesting. She wasn't an old maid. . . . Well, she was, I suppose, but she wasn't like one really."

"What did she look like?" asked Berger.

Without answering, Mrs Gibson got up and left the room. She was back before Green had lit a battered Kensitas, carrying several photographs. She handed each of the men two or three to look at.

"Why," said Berger, "she was a bit of all right."

"All right? She was lovely. A lot of people called her beautiful."

"How recently were these taken?" asked Green.

"All since she's been here—in the last three years."

"I was told she was forty."

"Forty-one, actually. She came here when she was thirty-eight."

"I'd like to keep one of these for a day or two," said Green. "I'd also like to know why a woman like her never married. I'd have thought she'd have had men buzzing round her like bees round a jampot."

"She was engaged once. To a right gay spark, I think."

"What happened?"

"He killed himself flying one of those little light aeroplanes. That's the sort he was, apparently. Fast cars, aeroplanes, speedboats . . . She didn't talk about him but I got the impression no man measured up to him afterwards."

"I see." Green put the photograph in his pocket.

DOUGLAS CLARK

"Now then, Mrs G., we've decided Miss Holland had no visitors. Not in the regular sense, that is. Could anybody have got in uninvited?"

Mrs Gibson shook her head. "The locals went all over the house. And it isn't as if we had these spring locks you can open with a bit of plastic. We've still got the old-fashioned ones from about seventy or eighty years ago."

"Mortise locks?"

"I don't know what that means, but I've got a big key that looks like a key to put in the keyhole, and that turns a tongue which goes into the doorjamb as solid as a rock."

"And the front door was locked when you came home?"

"Definitely. And the side door was bolted inside."

"What about the door into the school corridor?"

Mrs Gibson frowned. "I don't know. I didn't look."

"Why not?"

"Because we didn't worry about it much. I mean, the school was all locked up. I know the police checked that, so nobody could have got in that way."

Green did not comment for a moment, but then he asked: "If Miss Holland had rules about most things, why didn't she have one about that school door?"

"She did."

"But you can't say whether it would be locked or not?"

"Look, it wasn't locked normally. The keys are big old things and she didn't like carrying one about with her."

"Didn't she carry a handbag?" asked Berger.

"Not in school. She wore suits, with a pocket for a handkerchief. She thought it looked silly carrying a

56

handbag when wearing a gown. Besides, she wouldn't want things like lipstick and a comb while she was teaching. All that stuff was left in the little private cloakroom attached to her school study. It was a spare lot, of course. She left her bag in the house."

"So she left the house door unlocked so she could go to and fro without knocking or ringing?"

"In the daytime. Why not? It was only an internal door. We locked it at night of course. I did it, when I went round before bed. That's why I can't say whether it was locked or unlocked last night. I wasn't here to do it."

"Miss Holland didn't do the locking up herself, ever?"

"There was none to do except the school door, because we kept the front and side doors locked all the time."

"Very wise. Who opened the school door in the mornings?"

"I did. First thing—except Sundays—because Miss Holland would want to go out that way to Assembly. You see, I go into that passage every morning before breakfast for the apples."

"What apples?"

"She had one every morning for breakfast. She used to say they were a lot better than senna pods and a lot cheaper because they're grown here in the gardens. We put the apples down in a big old cupboard that's built in that little corridor. I go and get them every morning without fail."

"So the door was unlocked yesterday morning, but in all the fuss last night you didn't go there so you can't say whether the door was unlocked all evening or not."

"Does it matter? Nobody got in there. The locals went round the school. It was all locked up and nobody had broken in."

Green nodded to show he appreciated the point. Then he said: "You got home late from your day out, noticed the smell of vomit, found she'd been sick on the stairs . . ."

"Ever so sick. So I went up to her room. It was awful. She'd been sick again and the bedclothes were all scrumpled. I knew she was dead, of course, so I had to call the doctor, hadn't I?"

"Of course. He and the police searched the house?"

"That's right."

"And they asked you to stay on?"

"Well, I live here, don't I?"

"Yes, but . . ."

"Mr Hussey—he's the solicitor to the Board of Governors—asked me to stay on, in any case. This morning, that was. He said Miss Holland's stuff would have to be packed and the house would have to be kept up until a new headmistress came. She might want me or she might not, but they're going to pay my wages till they know."

"I see. That's nice for you." Green got to his feet. "Thank you, Mrs Gibson. Now, if Sergeant Berger could use your phone for a moment . . ."

"It's in her study. Just in front of this room. The light's just inside the door."

Berger left to call Masters.

Green said to the housekeeper: "Now, just one thing, Mrs G. Don't forget, tomorrow morning at the inquest, you're to make a point of saying how cheerful Miss Holland always was and particularly on the day she died."

"I'll not forget. I'm not having anybody saying she

did away with herself, 'cos she didn't. She had her head screwed on too well for that and she was a good lass. A right good, lovely lass."

For the first time since he arrived, Green saw tears brim in Mrs Gibson's eyes. Green patted her arm and led the way to the front door. Berger joined him in time to say goodbye to the housekeeper.

"They'll be here in a couple of minutes."

"Good. We'll wait outside on the road."

As Green lit another limp cigarette, Berger said: "She's a bit of an old gasbag—but nice with it."

"She's lonely and wanted somebody to talk to. She's missing her boss, that's what it is. Alone in a house where somebody's just died . . ."

CHAPTER III

"You were partly instrumental in getting us brought here, I understand, Sir Thomas."

Masters, tall and powerful, aggressively well-dressed in his grey, Windsor check suit and highly polished brown shoes, stood in the centre of a large and exquisite circular carpet. It was the centrepiece, dominating a room obviously richly furnished but without even the slightest hint of ostentation or vulgarity. It suggested—rather than displayed—a high degree of refined comfort which depended on heaviness, thickness and weight in its furnishings as much as on softness and shade. Sergeant Reed, also a tall man, but slight in comparison with Masters, stood beside their host and dwarfed him. And yet Kenny seemed to have a presence almost as commanding as that of the Superintendent.

"I was, and it frightens me," replied Kenny, indicating by a movement of a small hand holding a cigar that they should sit. As they sank into what felt like a sea of down, he continued: "Yes, it frightens me. On two counts. First, that had I not been convinced that Miss Holland would neither commit suicide nor be ignorant enough to make a fatal mistake such as the one that killed her, the local police would not have pursued the matter. And second, that had I not been

61

Chairman of the Watch Committee, they wouldn't have listened to me, anyway. I find it disturbing—if not worse."

"Whilst not being prepared to disagree, sir," replied Masters, smiling at the little man who seemed overwhelmed by the armchair he occupied, "I don't think you should either despair or cling to the idea that local police forces are inefficient in these rather odd cases. Almost inevitably, when one of them crops up, something happens to make the investigating officers pause and think again. This time it was you and—to be fair, Chief Superintendent Hildidge—who had doubts. Another time it could be an anonymous letter, a whisper from a contact or an unlikely coincidence which tips the scale. I am personally doubtful whether many cases are tackled in the wrong way. The fact that they are frequently not brought to a successful conclusion is a different matter."

"You think so?" asked Kenny sceptically.

"It must be so, sir. Take us as an example. We are here, now, investigating Miss Holland's death, and nobody can deny that we are presupposing murder. So we shall treat it as such. Nobody—including you, sir—will be able to say that we shall have neglected to treat it seriously, even thought we can give no guarantee of success in solving the problem."

"You're not trying to prepare me for failure, are you?"

"Far from it. I'm here to pick your brains and your memory with the intention of progressing towards an acceptable, proven solution. That is my aim."

"Have a cigar," said Kenny. "You're the sort of man I like. Here, Sergeant, help yourself."

"I'll stick to my pipe, sir, if I may," said Masters. "And I'd like to get down to business straight away."

...at what you think could happen?"
...a distinct possibility if what I have been told
..., and I have nothing with which to cause the
...r to hold his hand."
...ght. If that's how the wind blows, fire away.
...re had we got to?"
...ou said that Miss Holland's intention to resign
...s only partially true. Does that mean that as yet she
...s merely considering a move?"

"Yes."

"To better things?"

"I hoped so."

"My information leads me to believe that she had
...e to a definite conclusion in the matter."

"...h!"

...one so far as to inform you of her

"Good. You go ahead while I pour us a drink. Whisky will do for everybody, won't it?"

"The first question," said Masters, "is how did you hear of Miss Holland's death?" He was watching Kenny as he spoke and thought he detected a slight pause as their host tilted the decanter over an exquisitely cut pony-glass.

"I heard it from Raymond Hussey." He turned to carry two glasses to his guests. "Hussey is the school's solicitor as well as my own lawyer."

Masters accepted his glass.

"You were away on business?"

"Holiday."

"Where?"

"Just outside Guildford. No distance away."

"Your solicitor knew your address and movements?"

"No."

"Which means you rang him from your hotel near Guildford."

"Right." Kenny returned to the tray on the sideboard to pick up his own glass.

"When?"

"As soon as I'd finished breakfast this morning. Before half-past nine." When he was once again sitting in his armchair, he continued: "Mrs Gibson had rung the deputy headmistress earlier—at her home—to tell her the news. She naturally informed the Board's solicitor—at his home, before he left for his office."

"You rang before half-past nine," mused Masters. "Forgive me, Sir Thomas, but I find it strange that a man on holiday should have cause to ring his solicitor, particularly so early in the day, and then to discover that the call should be so fortuitous as it turned out to be."

"You're a smart man," said Kenny. "You're a suspicious one, too. Are you starting a case against me?"

"I think not. I've no wish to waste my time at the moment. So please tell me the circumstances in which you called Mr Hussey."

"Personal affairs."

"As opposed to business matters?"

"Quite. I was about to go off for the day, so I decided to call him before I went. It was that simple."

"What was your personal assessment of Miss Holland as a headmistress?" asked Masters, changing his line of questioning.

"Without a doubt, she was the best headmistress Bramthorpe ever had. A year or two ago, the school was beginning to slip from its former high standards, due to the present-day attitudes of the whole of this country. Miss Holland was appointed. Not only did she arrest the slide, but she had got the school back to the top of the hill. All in three years. Appointing her was the best bit of work the Governors had done in years."

"And your assessment of her as a person?"

"Marvellous. And lovely." He rose from his chair and crossed to a small bureau. From the top drawer he took a photograph wrapped in tissue paper. It was a large studio portrait, mounted on board and protected by a semi-opaque cover. "See for yourself." He handed the photograph to Masters.

"A beautiful woman, sir."

"Surprised?"

"A little. I must admit I had expected to see a picture of a strong character."

"But not one quite so good-looking."

"No, sir," confessed Masters.

Kenny took the photograph and returned it to the drawer. As he sat down again, he said: "So now you

can see why I could answe word: marvellous."

Masters sat back. "So what that Miss Holland was about to r

There was a long silence. At last

"How did you know that?" asked etly.

"It is true, then?"

"Partially."

"Please explain."

"You're a damn sight too perceptive for m said Kenny. "I don't know whether I feel sa. you about. You've been here in Bramthorpe no than a few hours and you are asking questions would never have occurred to Hildidge and his m

"I'm sorry to embarrass you

. . .I'm s. . . . . .you, but now seems as good
a time as any to remind you that you were largely
instrumental in bringing us here. I really do not feel
that you can complain of our methods or actions."

"I'm not complaining, dammit."

"No?"

"No. Just because I say you make me feel uncomfortable doesn't mean I'm complaining. Have you ever been questioned by a senior detective of your standing and acuity? I'll bet you haven't, so you don't know what it does to the one being interviewed, particularly if he's an old dictator like me who hasn't had a word of his questioned for years."

"I see, sir. I'm pleased you take it like that."

"Have I any choice?"

"Every choice. You are free to tell me to go to hell, in which case, tomorrow morning, a verdict of suicide or of accidental death could be brought in and it would then be felt, perhaps, that our services here would no longer be required."

"She hadn't gone so far decision?"

"I think you're barking up the wrong tree."

"Maybe. But I'm still gaining height."

"It was an ethical decision I was talking of."

"I think not. Ethical decisions tend to be hard, factual things. Not exciting or joyous to make. Yet Miss Holland had come to some momentous decision so exciting and joyous that she believed even her mother would be delighted by it."

Kenny nodded. "I'm pleased to hear it. But you said Miss Holland had decided to resign. I say she had not. It was an ethical decision she still had to make."

"Why ethical?" asked Reed. "Surely changing your job is not a matter of conscience as much as one of preference or opportunity or even, simply, of getting a bigger pay packet."

"True," agreed Kenny. "But the ethical question was a secondary consideration. As I said to Mr Masters, the problem had not been solved. But something else had been arranged."

"What?"

"A marriage."

"Miss Holland was about to get married?"

"That, I think, would be the news she was pleased about and you got wind of. You jumped to the conclusion that she had landed some job preferable even to the one she had here."

"I think I understand," said Masters. "Her ethical problem was whether, as a married woman, she could continue as headmistress of Bramthorpe and, presumably, instal her husband alongside her in the School House."

"The second part of that statement would not apply and the law would not allow the Governors to ask for her resignation just because she had married."

"Unless there is some provision in her agreement with the Board."

"Nothing like that."

"So how is her problem ethical? It is legal and in no way dubious."

Kenny grinned. "I was the fly in the ointment."

"You were objecting? You didn't want to lose . . . Wait a moment, sir. You're the man who thought she was so marvellous. And you are a widower. Was it you whom she was to marry?"

"That's it. She agreed to marry me only a week or so ago."

"What a tragedy this must have been for you, sir. I am extremely sorry."

"Thank you. I'm not over her loss by any means, but at my age . . . well, I'm not exactly a swooning young lover. I was shocked by the news, of course, but I felt more anger than any other emotion."

"That's why you insisted that Hildidge should not allow this matter to be dismissed as suicide or accidental death?"

"Of course. Think how well I knew her. Besides, I am convinced she was happy at the prospect of our marriage."

"I'm positive she was. Her letter to her mother showed that. She was keeping it as a precious, exciting secret to reveal to her family when she got home."

"Only to her mother. We decided to keep it quiet for a bit."

"Because of the ethical problem? What was it? Should she resign as headmistress so that you could continue as Chairman of the Board of Governors, or should you resign to allow her to stay on?"

"That's it. There were pros and cons on both sides. I wanted to resign because I felt the school needed her more than it did me. She said she wanted to be a real wife and run our home, with a bit of public work on the side. So she said she would resign. But her contract obliged her to give not only a term's notice, but a complete term's notice. That would mean waiting until next Easter to marry. But nothing was decided."

"Let's clear it all up, shall we?" asked Masters. "You had gone off on holiday immediately after becoming engaged to a woman who would herself be free for ten days as from this Friday. That doesn't ring true to me."

Kenny smiled. "I said you were too clever by half. Mabel had arranged to go to Malta for half term. I had arranged my own little break for this week. So where do you think I was going from Guildford on Saturday?"

"To Malta! I see. You weren't leaving here together

68

lest the gossip should start. So you hurriedly arranged to join her in Malta."

"At Heathrow. I even got a seat on the same plane."

"Right. Now the fortuitous call to your solicitor. An explanation for that, please, sir."

"I rang Mabel last evening. Naturally. She was alone in the house, ironing her smalls, getting her holiday things together and absolutely full of herself. She told me she was going to call in on Raymond Hussey this afternoon on school business and to ask him if he would take her on personally. Her previous man was in London, but she thought that if she was going to live in Bramthorpe for good, she would need a local man and it might as well be the chap who acted for me."

"She intended to tell Hussey that you two were engaged?"

"No, she couldn't do that because we were still undecided about our ethical problem and we reckoned it had better be worked out before the school solicitor got to hear the news."

"Why did you ring Hussey this morning?"

"Don't you see? When Mabel talked about both of us using Hussey, it reminded me that I would need to make a totally new will. So I spent last night thinking about it. And it occurred to me that they sometimes take these lawyers quite a long time to draw up. But I reckoned if Mabel decided to stay on at the school . . ."

"Persuaded by you whilst in Malta?"

"Right. Then there would be no reason for us to wait at all, and we could get married literally within days of our return. So I wanted the new will ready, just in case. So I rang Hussey to give him a sort of warning order. But I never got round to it. He told

me about Mabel's death and I came straight back to
Bramthorpe."

"I see, sir. Thank you."

"Anything else?"

"I'm afraid so."

"In that case we'll all have a refill. Sergeant, would
you act as duty steward?"

Reed got to his feet. Masters started to refill his
pipe.

"Thinking it out, are you?" asked Kenny.

Masters smiled. "No, sir. I know what I want to ask,
but there is something I want to say first. It's this.
Tomorrow Mrs Holland will be in Bramthorpe for
the inquest. Do you wish to meet her?"

"Yes."

"In what capacity? As Chairman of Bramthorpe
Governors or as the man who was to have married her
daughter?"

"I think the former. Nobody knows . . ."

"Just a moment, sir. Questions. You said earlier that
you and she had agreed to keep your engagement a
secret. Yet Miss Holland was patently intending to go
home to tell her mother before going off to Malta.
What near family have you got, sir?"

"A son. Married with two children."

"Have you told them?"

"With Mabel's permission, I told Norman and
Barbara immediately after she had consented to marry
me. We agreed to tell them and to ask them to keep
our secret. We both felt our close families had a right
to know. After all, we were doing nothing underhand,
but there were the reasons I've spoken about for not
going public."

"As far as I can make out, your secret has been kept.

The local police don't appear to know and neither, apparently, does your solicitor."

"That's why I think I'd better meet Mrs Holland in my capacity as Chairman."

"I think you're right, sir. The what-might-have-been could only add to her grief. Now, to come to my last point."

"What is it?"

"You said that Miss Holland had visited the solicitor, Hussey, on school business as well as to discuss her private affairs. Does that mean that the school was involved in some form of litigation that involved Miss Holland?"

"If you're looking for some malicious opponent in some legal suit, I'm afraid you'll be disappointed."

Masters replied blandly: "I shan't be disappointed, Sir Thomas, no matter what does or does not turn up."

"You mean it is all just a job of work to you?"

"Not quite. But a large amount of our work is nothing more than elimination. I must, obviously, ask about the solicitor because he was the only person we know of with whom she was about to have dealings. If what I learn about him and the nature of their business serves to eliminate Mr Hussey from further inquiries, I shall be a step further forward in my investigation."

"Heads I win, tails you lose?"

"Something of the sort. But you seem reluctant to tell me about the visit to the school's solicitor."

"Which makes you suspicious?"

"A little. If you persist, I can only become more so."

Kenny thought for a moment before replying.

"The reason why I haven't rushed to tell you about Mabel's proposed visit to Hussey is, I suppose, because

71

DOUGLAS CLARK

I thought it would lead you astray by directing your attention to a man whom I have known for a great many years and who—in my opinion—could not possibly be considered as one of your suspects."

"Sir," said Reed, "doing a cover-up job on somebody is not helpful to that person. It heightens the suspicion."

"I know that now, Sergeant. I'm an old fool, I suppose. So I'll tell you. Hussey wasn't feeling very pleased with Mabel."

"As a headmistress?"

"No, no. He thought she was wonderful in that area. The point is, the school has never had a bursar. Nobody had ever felt the need for one, as Hussey's firm did it all for us. They sent out the school bills and collected in the money. They did the accounts, paid the rates, saw to tenders for painting and building. I think it all stemmed from some notion way back that such things were not fit work for women, but one couldn't have a male bursar in a girls' school."

"Hussey did all this as well as acting as Secretary to the Board of Governors?"

"Yes. All very cosy, isn't it?"

"Presumably it has worked well?"

"Very well."

"And Hussey has enjoyed the business?"

"It has been one of his firm's traditional mainstays."

"So what has happened?"

"Mabel wished to appoint a bursar."

"Ah! Wasn't she satisfied with Hussey? Had he grown too expensive?"

"Mabel was a good administrator, as well as being a great teacher. She felt the need to hold the reins, but I doubt whether she would have made the move

72

to take over completely had it not been for Miss Lickfold.

"Miss Lickfold is the longest serving mistress at the school and was, at the time of Mabel's appointment, deputy headmistress. She is now within a year or two of retirement. Mabel's predecessor left the school because of illness. Miss Lickfold took over, in the interregnum, until a new head could be appointed. I need hardly tell you that Miss Lickfold applied for the job and fully expected to get it."

"But the board thought otherwise?"

"She had no support. We were unanimous that she would have been hopeless. We knew little of her teaching ability, but we did know she was more like a Victorian governess than a modern schoolteacher. We dare not have entrusted Bramthorpe to her."

"So there was bad blood between Miss Lickfold and Miss Holland."

"I don't think so. But there was a keen sense of disappointment on Miss Lickfold's side and an even keener sense of Miss Lickfold's inadequacy as a teacher on Mabel's side."

"Ah!"

"It took Mabel less than a term to realise that her senior assistant was not up to her job. At the school, it has been traditional for the senior forms to be taught exclusively by the more senior mistresses and the junior school by the junior mistresses. So Miss Lickfold was only teaching her subjects to the Lower and Upper Fifths and the Sixth form."

"The most important forms—those preparing for extra-mural exams?"

"Right. Mabel was very hot on her timetable being adhered to and that upper school teaching should be geared exclusively to examination syllabuses. In order to learn what was going on, when she first arrived, she did spot-checks on the girls' exercise books. She soon discovered that Miss Lickfold was going into form rooms for specific lessons, but was, as often as not, merely discussing whatever subject entered her head. For instance, instead of setting written prep in History one night, she had told the Upper Fifth to write an essay on euthanasia. When Mabel spotted this she was very perturbed on several counts. First, she was angry that a mistress should waste the time of girls preparing for a specific exam. Second, she was even more angry to learn that Miss Lickfold had spent that day's History period discussing euthanasia instead of Palmerston or some such thing. Third, she was of the opinion that healthy-minded fifteen and sixteen-year-old girls should not be subjected at any time to lessons on so morbid and unsuitable a subject. Fourth, she was worried because Miss Lickfold lived with her elderly mother who had been a chronic invalid—bed-ridden—for many years. Miss Lickfold supported her mother most dutifully, but Mabel was afraid lest Miss Lickfold's preoccupation with euthanasia should have a sinister and personal basis."

"What did Miss Holland do about it?"

"At first she proposed to wait until the end of that first term and then to rejig the timetable. Meanwhile she was wondering how best to warn Miss Lickfold—without hurting any feelings—that the syllabus must be adhered to. Then came another incident which I understand was typical of the woman. If there was talking in the form room and she was unable to detect the culprit, her ploy was to pick on some innocent girl and say, 'Mary Jones, you are talking.' When the girl replied, 'No, Miss Lickfold,' the old trout would reply, 'Well you are now. Do fifty lines on Walpole as a punishment for contradicting.' As you can imagine, such treatment was unlikely to be tolerated by today's sixteen-year-olds, though they seem to have put up with it for long enough. But, as I say, shortly after the euthanasia business, Mabel had a complaint from a parent whose daughter had been unjustly punished. The parent had investigated the affair before approaching Mabel."

"What did Miss Holland do about it?"

"She acted immediately. By introducing a punishment book. Any punishment given in the school had to be entered in the book. This was no trouble, because with the other mistresses punishments—in senior forms particularly—were very few and far between and had to be well-merited. Mabel herself interviewed each girl involved before the task was done. Her excuse was that she wanted to identify the troublemakers and naughty ones. The reasonable mistresses understood what was going on and welcomed it. It gave Mabel the means to stop any further foolishness on Miss Lickfold's part."

"It seems to have been a very diplomatic way of handling the situation."

"Mabel felt she was in a difficult position. The Lickfold was a beaten rival for the headship, and she felt the need to handle the woman with kid gloves. She changed staff responsibilities at the end of the term and relieved Miss Lickfold of her senior school duties. Actually, Mabel would have liked to be rid of her, but short of criminal misdemeanour there is no way of sacking such a teacher these days, and, in any case, Lickfold was supporting a sick mother. But of late— and I'm talking, I suppose, about the last two summers and their exams—Mabel had been achieving excellent results with the upper school. To improve still further, she realised that the standard of teaching in the lower school had to be brought up to the same level as that in the top forms."

"To give the girls a good, solid grounding?"

"Right."

"And Miss Lickfold was again the culprit?"

"The chief of them. But as I said, there's no easy way of getting rid of a duff teacher and Mabel was, in any case, very conscious of Miss Lickfold's private responsibilities. So she had thought up a solution that corresponded with her wish to get the administration of the school's affairs into her own hands. It was to offer Miss Lickfold the post of first Bursar of Bramthorpe. She made the offer last Easter. It had an added inducement for Lickfold were she to accept the offer. She would be allowed to work until she was sixty-five. That would give her five more years of salary with an increased pension to follow."

"A reasonable proposal for somebody with an expensive dependent, one would suppose. How did Miss Lickfold view it?"

"Not surprisingly, she was attracted by it, but said she felt the school could not do without her teaching ability and experience. So she suggested a compromise—that she should become bursar after she had reached the age of retirement from teaching."

"Thought she was indispensable, did she? What was Miss Holland's reaction?"

"Simply to tell her that a bursar would be appointed this last September and that the post and its benefits would not be there for her when she wanted it. That did the trick. The senior maths mistress, Miss Bulmer, was appointed deputy headmistress and Miss Lickfold took up her duties—nominally—as bursar."

"And it was in this connection that Miss Holland

76

had proposed to visit Hussey this afternoon, had she been alive to do so?"

"That's right. Of course, a department like a bursar's office takes some time to establish properly, and Mabel was faced with the task of prising all but the actual legal business out of Hussey's hands."

"He didn't want to let it go?"

"He has been dragging his feet. Always with an apparently good excuse, of course. The affairs were a bit widespread. An accounts clerk had the school bills, the conveyancing man had the deeds of the school and the three boarding houses. Hussey himself had the board's minutes and all the contracts. According to Mabel who was, I may tell you, a very precise and neat administrator, Hussey's handling of our affairs reminded her more of a kitten's efforts with a ball of wool than a well-regulated business house."

"Could it be that her knowledge of how ill-conducted Hussey's business appeared to be helped Miss Holland to come to her decision to instal a bursar?"

"I would say it had a lot to do with it. Which bird came first—Hussey's slipshod methods or Miss Lickfold's inadequacies—I can't be sure, but Mabel was intent on using the one stone to kill the two."

"How did Hussey take it when Miss Holland suggested to the board that a bursar should be appointed? I presume that, as secretary to the governors, he was present?"

"He didn't like the idea."

"But the board members did?"

"All of us. I've no doubt whatsoever that Mabel had done a bit of lobbying before the meeting. It was easy for her, really. The three women governors were all for having a woman administrator instead of leaving it in the hands of a man, and as for the male members of the board . . . Well, Mabel was a very attractive, persuasive woman. And, in any case, when it came to the day-to-day running of the school, we rarely thwarted the wishes of the headmistress, particularly those of so able a headmistress as Mabel."

"So today, Miss Holland was to have visited Hussey to make sure that everything which should have been handed over had, in fact, been given to the new bursar?"

"That was just like Mabel. She wouldn't have left it to a subordinate to do the dirty work."

"Meaning there was a degree of ill feeling on Hussey's part? Otherwise the task would not have been unpleasant?"

"Raymond Hussey can be a bit mean-minded."

"Yet Miss Holland proposed to put her own affairs in his hands. Is he the only trustworthy solicitor in Bramthorpe?"

"Apart from the fact that it would be useful for her, as my wife, to use the same man, it was to soften the blow. To give him at least a bit of something by way of recompense for removing so much of the school business."

"That reply indicates that Miss Holland was aware that she was not exactly Hussey's favourite headmistress."

"You could put it that way."

"I think I must, don't you, Sir Thomas? We are presuming somebody bore her sufficient ill will to poison her. We must consider, therefore, both Miss Lickfold, who may be feeling aggrieved because she lost the headship to Miss Holland who then dealt blows to her pride by removing her first from the senior school and then from teaching altogether, and also Mr Hussey who is less than pleased with losing a slice of lucrative business."

Kenny got to his feet, clearly ill at ease. Then he said: "I feel terrible about this. It's as though I had delivered those two people into your hands."

"No, sir. Nobody has delivered anybody into my hands. I am looking round. Nothing more."

Before Kenny could reply, the phone rang.

Masters was quite happy to tell Green that he and Reed would be round at the school to pick him and Berger up in no time at all.

They sat up late in Masters' room. Each pair reported fully on their respective interviews. After some discussion, Green said: "So it looks as though there are three possibilities on the list so far."

"Three?" asked Berger. "How do you make that out? The Lickfold woman. She had a grudge—hurt dignity—and it's quite feasible to suppose she could potter round to the School House to see Miss Holland. All of a doodah to see if the headmistress was going to get what she wanted out of that nasty Mr Hussey. And while she was there, she could have off-loaded a handful of laburnum seeds into something . . ."

"Like what?" asked Reed.

"Oh . . . the fried mushrooms or tomatoes or whatever. That's not my point. Then there's Hussey. He'd have a good excuse for calling round. 'Oh, Miss Holland, I know you're coming to see me tomorrow, but I think I ought to mention that your new bursar is really falling down on the job. I've been informed that the second half of the school rates are overdue and if they're not paid by midday tomorrow at the latest there'll be a summons taken out against you.' "

Berger turned to Masters. "You know the sort of thing, Chief. He's invited in for sherry and palms the seeds into something . . ."

"Like what?" asked Reed again.

Berger shrugged. "The exact method is not what I'm talking about. The D.C.I. said three suspects. I'm saying there's only two as far as I can see."

Reed shook his head in sorrow. "You should know by now that murder, like charity, begins at home. It's a family affair more often than not."

"Miss Holland hadn't any family."

"She had a housekeeper—same thing."

"Who was out all day."

"Still . . ."

"If you'd seen her and talked to her, you wouldn't suspect Mrs Gibson."

"Well, now . . ."

"Yes?"

"What about that deep custard we've heard about? With nutmeg on top? Who made that? And how do we know the coarsely ground nutmeg wasn't coarsely ground laburnum seeds all baked in the pie?"

"It couldn't have been."

"Why not?"

"Because Mrs Gibson ate it up herself."

"Did she? Was there any left for us to send for testing?"

"No."

"There wouldn't be, would there? Not if she disposed of it as soon as she could after she got home last night. I reckon a deep custard would go down a drain. The innards would slither down and the crust could be broken up to go through the grid."

Berger looked across at Green. "Is that what you meant?"

"That's it, laddie. Like you, I think Mrs Gibson is a genuine old trout, but we've got to bear all the possibilities in mind."

Masters got to his feet. "We'll call it a day. I want to make some notes for tomorrow."

"You're still set on appearing?"

"Yes."

"Shall you approach the coroner beforehand?"

"I think I'd better. I don't know whether he is one of those who has his witness list made up before he opens and then doesn't stray from it, or whether he is one who will hear anybody who has—or thinks he has—anything to contribute. So I'll make sure. I'll ask to appear last. I want Mrs Gibson's evidence to be heard before mine. And I've had another thought."

"What's that?"

"Because I want to use the contents of that letter from her daughter, I would like formal permission from Mrs Holland to represent her. That would give me the right to appear if Gilchrist raises any objections to two police witnesses."

"I should say there'll be no difficulty in getting Mrs Holland to agree, judging by her co-operative attitude when I spoke to her over the phone."

"Good. You're arranging to have her met. Can I leave it to you to fix that, too—just in case I'm otherwise engaged?"

"Leave it to me."

CHAPTER IV

Dr Gilchrist, the coroner, was a tall, spare man, dressed in a navy-blue suit with a chalk stripe. He wore a waistcoat, a semi-stiff collar and a club tie. His face was jowled and high-coloured; his hair grey and sleeked down; his spectacles gold-rimmed. Impeccable: no-nonsense. He gave the impression that he regarded the inquest as a job to be done well and with dispatch. Before the court opened he had listened gravely to Masters' request to appear as a private individual representing Mrs Holland. He had disapproved, but conceded that he was in duty bound to hear all that was relevant to the case before him unless the Bramthorpe police were to ask for an adjournment, in which case he could conceivably curtail the hearing without calling Masters.

Masters would have welcomed an adjournment, because he liked neither the idea of appearing himself nor of parading evidence in public before he had been given the time to build his case. But he was certain that D.I. Lovegrove would not ask directly for an adjournment nor would he present his evidence in such a way as to suggest to Gilchrist that it would be desirable to allow the police more time. This being so, Masters was not prepared to risk an unfavourable verdict being brought in because of a lack of evidence from the locals and for the want of intervention on his own part.

Evidence of identification by two mistresses from the senior school staff. Evidence of cause of death from the Bramthorpe Hospital pathologist. Cytisine, a highly toxic alkaloid found in laburnum and some other leguminous plants. Resembles nicotine in its actions. Toxic effects include nausea and vomiting (Miss Holland had vomited massively), dilatation of the pupils and tachycardia—the coroner himself would know that tachycardia means abnormal rapidity of the heart's action—followed by dizziness, mental confusion (which probably accounted for Miss Holland not telephoning for help), muscular inco-ordination and weakness (probably accounting for why she neither undressed before lying down nor managed to make her way to a bathroom or lavatory to vomit), followed by convulsions (which would account for the bedraggled state of the bed-clothes) followed by respiratory paralysis leading to death by asphyxia—which though literally meaning stoppage of the pulse, could be interpreted as suffocation produced by a deficiency of oxygen in the blood.

The amount of laburnum seeds? Probably a level tablespoonful. As many as that? It was an estimate, but —if the coroner would forgive the term—an educated estimate, arrived at scientifically.

Laburnum? Could the pathologist tell the court anything of the plant itself?

Certainly. Commonly called Golden Rain. Green, trifoliate leaves on long stalks; golden yellow flowers with five petals, unequal in size—hence the name Golden Rain—hanging from the branches on long racemes —like bunches of grapes—seen in May and June; fruit pod has eight seeds which become dark brown when ripe. Seldom grows wild. Commonly cultivated. All parts poisonous, particularly bark and seeds. Laburnum causes the greatest number of cases of poisoning and death in man in Britain at present time. Children eat seeds in mistake for peas. Animals have also been poisoned. Seeds, wood, bark and roots of tree are consistently toxic.

Gilchrist thanked the pathologist who then stepped down.

Mrs Gibson. As expected, she had no light to throw on the tragedy, but she was duly led through her story, stressing, as she went, how level-headed, cheerful and happy Miss Holland had been right up to the last moment Mrs Gibson had seen her.

Fellows, the chemist, and his girl assistant both to report that Miss Holland had bought merely items for her holiday trip and had certainly not asked for any substance or medicament that was in the least toxic, that she had seemed happy and cheerful and not in the least depressed.

Masters began to feel slightly better about things. Gilchrist was apparently examining his witnesses with a view to scotching a suicide verdict. There remained only D.I. Lovegrove before he himself expected to be called.

It was Masters' first sight of the local detective inspector. He was rather fleshy—thick of lip and neck. But smart in appearance and well-prepared in what he was saying. Glib? Masters found it hard to decide. Any police officer who did not prepare his spiel before appearing as a witness was a bit of a fool. But Lovegrove? Joe Smoothie of the year? Green evidently thought so. He grimaced and nudged Masters. "He's got it all off pat, hasn't he?" he whispered.

Lovegrove was pressing hard for a verdict of accidental death. There was no evidence to show that any second person had been in the School House that evening. There was no hint as to how a second person could have administered a large number of laburnum seeds to Miss Holland, either secretly or overtly. There had certainly been no struggle. Miss Holland had sustained no injuries, as she most certainly would have done had she tried to fight off another person intent on poisoning her. In addition to a conspicuous lack of either opportunity or means, there was no indication—despite careful investigation of this point by himself and his officers—of any ill will towards the deceased such as might constitute a motive for causing Miss Holland harm. Indeed, she was so popular and highly respected a person that it had proved impossible to find anybody who had wished her other than well.

Green grunted angrily as Lovegrove had his say and then answered the few questions put to him. As Lovegrove stepped down, the D.C.I. said hoarsely: "It's up to you, George. That bastard thinks it's all over bar the shouting."

It caused a stir in the court when Gilchrist called Masters. Lovegrove, who hadn't, by then, regained his seat, stopped and turned round in amazement. Then he stepped back into the aisle to confront Masters.

"You didn't let us know you intended to appear," he said.

"Sir!" reminded Masters blandly.

"Sir."

"And you hadn't the courtesy to make yourself known to me, Mr Lovegrove. Had you done so, we might have compared notes."

"Superintendent," called Gilchrist petulantly, "the court is waiting."

"My apologies, sir. I was unexpectedly . . . er . . . accosted."

Masters strode forward, a huge man in an impeccable suit and highly polished shoes. He carried a buff folder which he put on the shelf inside the box before looking up to face Gilchrist.

"I understand, Superintendent, that you feel you have something to contribute to this hearing."

"If you please, sir."

"I understand also that you have been brought from Scotland Yard to investigate this case, yet the police evidence has been given by Detective Lovegrove. Why is that?"

"Because, sir, I arrived only very late in the day. Sometime after teatime yesterday. Between then and now it has proved impossible—in view of this inquest and the fact that D.I. Lovegrove was not available to see me when I arrived—for me to get very far with my inquiries."

"If you have no case to present to this court, why do you wish to appear?"

"To acquaint you with the circumstances leading to the request for help from Scotland Yard and to present some facts not yet mentioned."

"A second set of police evidence, then?"

"Not formally, sir. I am appearing, by your courtesy, as a private individual, at least in part."

"You have a personal interest in the case?"

"In so far as I am representing Mrs Holland, the deceased's mother, in your court, sir."

"This could be highly irregular."

"With respect, sir, I think not. Even though I am a police officer, I have the same rights as any other citizen and hence am not precluded from appearing in any capacity or even in a dual role."

The coroner considered this for a moment.

"Very well. Carry on. I will decide whether to include or exclude what you have to say after I have heard it."

Masters inclined his head.

"Yesterday morning, after the circumstances of Miss Holland's death were known, two people made representations to the Chief Constable concerning it. One was Sir Thomas Kenny who, as Chairman of the Board of Governors of Bramthorpe College, knew Miss Holland extremely well. He gave it as his opinion that Miss Holland was the reverse of suicidal and that he, for one, could not accept that she had taken her own life."

"Sir Thomas Kenny approached the police to say this?"

"As Chairman of the Watch Committee, he felt it his duty to return from holiday to make his opinion known in person."

"And the second representation?"

"Came from Chief Superintendent Hildidge, the senior police officer of Bramthorpe. He has been involved for many years in dealing with cases of violent and unnatural death, and is, consequently, more aware than most men that it is impossible to say who is, and who is not, a suicidal type. And yet he felt so strongly that Miss Holland—with whom he was well acquainted—would not in any circumstances take her own life that, despite his great knowledge and experience, he made his opinion known to his superior officer."

"Yet the local C.I.D. were inquiring into the death?"

"Quite so, sir. But as a result of the representations I have mentioned, I was asked to come to Bramthorpe to head an investigation."

"Thank you, Superintendent. The court now knows why you are here. But, so far, you have shed no light on the mystery surrounding the death of the deceased. We have heard opinions only. I would prefer facts."

"You shall have facts. But may I respectfully remind you, sir, that at this stage in the proceedings, opinions may be of value?"

"I am aware, Superintendent, that this is not a trial and that the court is required to reach an opinion. But that opinion will be based on fact. So may we now stop the verbal sparring and come to what you have to say?"

Masters waited for just a moment before continuing. He had to judge whether, in the face of what Gilchrist had just said, he could afford to pursue the line of argument he had prepared. As the coroner looked up to question the delay, Masters decided to stick to his guns.

"It is a fact, sir, that you as a medical man will have called for, or even been asked to give, a second opinion. Diagnosis and action follow opinion. May I suggest that the problem of Miss Holland's death is a case where a somewhat similar procedure must be followed? Fact number one is this letter . . ."

"Facts at last, Mr Masters?"

"As promised, sir. It is a letter written by Miss Holland to her mother who received it on the day of her daughter's death. In it, Miss Holland revealed that she had some wonderful news which she knew would delight her mother."

"What news?"

"The news was unspecified, sir, but Miss Holland obviously regarded it as so momentous that she had intended to visit her mother to impart it in person. Perhaps you would care to read the letter yourself?"

Gilchrist held out his hand and the court attendant carried the letter across to him. He spent a minute or so reading the neat, legible writing, and then turned to his jury and read the relevant passage to them. Then he turned back to Masters, who continued his statement.

"I have produced this letter, sir, on behalf of Mrs Holland and as an indication to you of the frame of mind of the deceased only a day or so before her death."

"Quite. I should be very interested to know what the momentous news was. Are you sure you are in no position to enlighten me?"

"Mrs Holland confesses she has no inkling, and I would suggest that if the deceased was too thrilled with her news to tell it to her own mother in a letter, then she could well have kept it a secret from others until the appropriate time came."

"You've had no time to investigate this?"

"I have not yet had time even to visit the School House, sir. But I did learn of the existence of this letter, and its contents caused me to believe that Miss Holland did not take her own life."

"I accept that it is a strong pointer to support the opinion you have been so insistent on."

Masters bowed his head slightly as if in acknowledgment of the fact that Gilchrist had dismissed the idea of suicide. Then he spoke again.

"Fact number two, sir, is Miss Holland's wide knowledge of the biological science."

"How does that affect the issue?"

"Her academic qualifications enabled her to teach, to a high level, subjects concerning plants and plant life. She was in fact a botanist. She would, I suggest, be able to identify laburnum seeds and would be very well aware of their toxic qualities."

Gilchrist sat back from his writing and eyed Masters keenly. "I am beginning to be very interested, Superintendent."

"Thank you, sir. Fact number three is that nowhere in the school grounds is there a laburnum tree. I imagine the absence of such a tree was a deliberate precaution on the part of those who laid out and planted the school's flora many years ago."

"What significance do you attach to such an absence, Mr Masters?"

"Simply that if there are no laburnum trees in or near the school, sir, then the seeds must have been carried there by somebody for some purpose."

"Go on."

"I find it hard to envisage the headmistress of Bramthorpe deliberately setting out to locate a laburnum tree and to collect the seeds."

"Perhaps for tutorial purposes?"

"You may be right, sir, but there are reasons why I would question that. Miss Holland has been described to me as a meticulous headmistress. I cannot see a woman who has charge of three hundred girls and who knows the potential danger of laburnum seeds introducing them to her school. Even were she to do so, so conscientious a woman would make immediate provision for their destruction after use, or for their keeping to be so safe that all possibility of accident can be discounted. But, sir, I venture to suggest that a woman such as Miss Holland would not keep dangerous seeds for several months . . ."

"Several months, Mr Masters? How can you suggest such a time?"

"Whilst I admit this period is pure supposition, if one considers the growing season of the laburnum ... The court has heard how its flowers appear relatively early in the year, in May and June. By July the seed pods have formed. By August they have ripened. By September they have fallen and are gone, sir, lost in long grass, carried off by birds, eaten by slugs ... certainly not there for easy collecting in great numbers."

"I take the point, Mr Masters."

"In that case, sir, may I suggest that in the light of how little we know of this case, as yet, it would be premature to return a verdict of accidental death or of suicide? Miss Holland was too knowledgeable to suggest the former without positive proof of accident, and too stable and happy to suggest the latter."

"I have one question, Mr Masters."

Masters waited.

"You have led the court to believe that you are of the opinion that Miss Holland did not collect the laburnum seeds herself. What are we to assume from that?"

"I am obliged—for the purposes of my investigation—to bear in mind the strong possibility that they were collected and carried to the School House, at some time previous to the hour at which Miss Holland was poisoned, by another person. I must also consider that a degree of malice was the cause of ..."

Gilchrist held up his hand.

"I'll stop you there, Mr Masters. As you will know, a Coroner's jury cannot now bring in a specific criminal charge, so it would be as well if the members were to consider what you have said so far without learning details of what must be, at this stage, merely your working hypothesis."

e school captain and one or two other prefects to
heir views. Between us we might turn something

een turned to the sergeants. "Watch it, you two.
e of these eighteen-year-olds are hot stuff and the
that goes to schools like Bramthorpe isn't as in-
ed as you might think."

rger grinned. "Jealous?"

Vhy not? I'd rather get into a huddle with a few
lass bits of capurtle than some school secretary."

he may be a smasher."

et's hope so," retorted Green.

it was Thursday, a day on which there was no
noon school, the sergeants had to accompany
ers and Green to get the names and addresses of
prefects from the secretary.

ne large double gates at the downhill end of the
ol were open. Reed drove the Rover through them
the concrete. Masters walked towards the first
e doors in his wing of the school. Green caught
up. "There's a bell on the post."

nd also two very discreet notices. 'Secretary' and
of bounds to pupils'."

eculiar, that. The kids have to go through the two
le doors."

o hang up their coats and to change into house-
"

ouseshoes?"

ttle, light, indoor shoes. Establishments like this
allow three hundred girls to clomp around in
outdoor, wooden-soled wedges. Too noisy, too
and too dangerous."

uppose you had to wear houseshoes?"

ost definitely. And they weren't allowed to have
soles."

"I had finished what I wished to say to the court,
sir. As you know, my investigation has not yet started,
so I can give no evidence which suggests categorically
that there will be a criminal case to answer. All I am
seeking to do is to help the court not to arrive at
what may be an incorrect verdict simply because we
have not so far had an opportunity to make our inquiries."

"You would prefer a verdict that would leave you
free to pursue your investigations?"

"If you find it possible, sir."

Masters returned to his seat.

"Just the hammer," said Green. "He can't tie us
down now."

A few minutes later an open verdict was returned.

Hildidge said: "I heard most of what you had to say."

Masters, sitting with Green, opposite to the local
Chief Superintendent in his office, asked: "You came
along for the show?"

"Lovegrove radioed in when he knew you were appearing. He was in a bit of a tizzy, so I went across to
listen. It's so close by that I only missed a minute or
two."

"Why should he be worried?" asked Green.

"I was, too, to begin with."

"Why?"

"I thought Mr Masters might be setting out to
make us look a proper load of Charlies."

Masters stretched his legs. "Nothing was further
from my mind. I took the decision last night—to take
the stand this morning—and I came over here early to
meet Lovegrove and let him know and to discuss the
matter. But he was not here. I asked for you too, sir,
to let you know, but I was told you were discussing the

safety arrangements for the town bonfire with the Bramthorpe P.R.O."

"I'm pleased I was. If you'd told me of your intentions I'd have been obliged to let Lovegrove know. As it was, I could truthfully claim I knew nothing about it and couldn't be considered guilty of non-cooperation."

"He accused you of that?" asked Green.

"He suspects me of it. The fact that we brought you here hasn't helped our relationship."

"Never mind," said Green. "Discover there are a few dogs gone missing. That should keep him busy."

"As I had no opportunity to consult with Lovegrove," said Masters, "I literally had to appear."

"I know," said Hildidge. "But Lovegrove would never have seen the paradox. He was content to say there were, apparently, no means, opportunities or motives, but he couldn't accept that there was every reason to suppose it was neither suicide nor accident. I'm pleased you put it to the coroner. I wouldn't have wanted Dr Gilchrist to have come out of it with egg on his face. He's not the sort to forget—had he brought in suicide or accident and you proved different—that he'd based the wrong findings on Lovegrove's negative evidence."

"So everybody except Lovegrove is happy," said Green. "It's too bad about him."

"I liked the point," said Hildidge, "when you hinted that if somebody else had collected those seeds it couldn't have been an accident."

"I hope I didn't overdo it. But you see, sir, I was obsessed by the thought that only a botany mistress would collect laburnum seeds in the normal course of events. Nobody else would. Or if they would, I couldn't

imagine why they should. And Miss Holla[nd] one and only botany mistress around. So a[ny] picking them up and carrying them to House must have a funny reason for doing

"You didn't overplay it. Gilchrist got it. that matters. Now what?"

"To work," said Masters. "We have one o[f] quiries to make."

Hildidge smiled. "I'll bet. You're the type make bricks without straw. Lord knows what age when somebody delivers you a few bale[s] with."

"We make corn-dollies," said Green. "We'l[l] have one for your sideboard."

As they sat at lunch, eating devilled kidneys said: "It was a good show you put up this m[orning] George. The only question is, how are we g[oing to] follow it?"

"So far, I must admit, I've concentrated so m[uch on] that damned inquest that I'm not at all sure want to proceed. So, we'll cast our bread."

"Where?"

"How about in two directions to begin with and I can see the school secretary to see if anything we should know about Miss Holland th[at] Thomas and Mrs Gibson haven't told us. What is, they obviously thought the sun shone out Would an employee take the same view?"

"On the principle that no man is a hero to man?"

"Quite. And in the same context, Reed an can locate some of the senior girls—the sensi[ble] and see what they thought of her. I suggest

"Why not?"

"Black soles mark oak blocks and terrazzo—the way kids kick and dance about."

Green grunted and stuck out a stubby forefinger to press the bell. They heard no sound of ringing, but after a moment or two they sensed movement and then the door was opened.

"I would like to speak to the school secretary, please," said Masters.

"Speaking. And I know who you are. I saw you at the inquest this morning."

"You were there, Miss . . . ?"

"Freeman. Yes, I was there. Miss Bulmer—she's the deputy headmistress—told me to go along with Mrs Gibson, just in case, you know."

"Very thoughtful of Miss Bulmer," replied Masters. "This is Detective Chief Inspector Green. He and I would like to talk to you. Sergeant Reed and Sergeant Berger would like some names and addresses from you."

"You'd better come in, then."

There had obviously been changes in the structure and the use of this area of the school. There were modern skirting-boards and lights, patently newish flush doors and, indeed, what Masters took to be false, lower ceilings.

He looked about him as they followed Miss Freeman. She was a big woman, heavily built. He judged she was the type that had to be careful what she ate if she wasn't to run to fat. As it was, her legs and hands were pudgy and her cheeks well-rounded. Her hair was still brown for the most part, but it was greying at the temples. Her eyes gave an impression of bewildered kindness. He guessed the death of the headmistress had knocked her off her perch and left her—temporarily, at least—somewhat aimless.

"Oh yes," she said when he remarked that there appeared to have been alterations made. "In the old days the school used to have all sorts of odd classes like Housewifery and Home Management. We still do cookery, of course, but in the old days they used to teach the senior girls how to bath babies and all that sort of thing. They used big dolls and those awful old zinc baths. And household accounts and all sorts of sewing like drawn-thread work and samplers. Tatting even. When I first came here I found a box full of tatting shuttles.

"Anyhow, a new domestic science area was opened up in the top wing years before the war, and all those horrible old black gas stoves and laundry sinks were taken out down here. That was at the time when the school first got a secretary. Before my time, of course. But to the right there you'll see the dining room and beyond it the kitchen. That was the old cookery room."

"Pretty small for three hundred kids," said Green.

"It's not for three hundred. All the boarders have lunch in their own houses. Most of the other girls go home for lunch. This dining room is only for long-distance travellers and school teams on match days."

"I see. Sorry."

"I'm just around to the left here, below the steps. They go up to the library and the cloakrooms. There are a lot of steps about, you'll find, because we are built on the side of a hill."

Masters made no effort to interrupt Miss Freeman, guessing that the chance to talk was what she needed most at this time. Even Green didn't seem bored.

"And it was at that time that the headmistress first

got a school study—as well as the one in her house. It's just along here." She moved past the end of the corridor leading to the cloakrooms. "It's a suite, really. I was told there used to be two rooms here for really little girls—a sort of preparatory division—not for boarders, of course. But you could only get into the back room through the front one. And it is that back one which is now the school study. They gave it its own little corridor, you see, by taking off a bit of the front room. The rest of the room was divided into two. The bit that overlooks the quad is the head's private cloakroom, and the rest is the book store—because it didn't have to have any windows, you see."

As she finished speaking she led them down the little corridor and opened the study door. It was big for a study, perhaps, but must have been very small for a schoolroom. The two long multi-paned windows looked out onto the perfectly cut grass of the quad. Opposite the door was an open fireplace. Miss Holland obviously liked this behind her desk chair. The light from the windows came in over the left-hand end of her desk, so that she sat facing the door.

She also sat facing the school clock.

It was a handsome piece of workmanship, hanging on the wall. A long drop-case clock, electric, with two faces. The upper one was normal enough. The lower one was a bright brass disc of the same size, but it had no hands. It was divided into twenty-four hours, but was pierced by a great many holes to take small brass pegs.

"What on earth is that?" asked Green. "It looks like an automated crib board."

"It controls all the clocks and bells in the school. It is the master, and all the clocks keep exactly the same time as this. So if there's a power cut or something, the only one that has to be put right is this. The pegs are to set off the bells at the right time for changing periods. They can be changed, you see, but they never were. Every period was just three-quarters of an hour, and they stopped and started at the same time every day. But you can see there were no lessons on Tuesday, Thursday and Saturday afternoons, or Sundays, of course."

"You mean that thing controls for a full week?"

"It has to, otherwise we'd be for ever switching it on and off, or bells would be ringing in an empty school. No, we only ever switch off for holidays."

"I see. It's a nice room."

"Yes. And in normal times it always has cut flowers or bowls of bulbs. I get them from the head grounds-man."

Masters stood by the window. "Miss Freeman, I would like to ask you just a few questions, but first I would like my sergeants to have the addresses I mentioned. How many houses are there? Not boarding houses, but school divisions?"

"Four."

"Thank you. Could we have the names and addresses of the school captain—if that is what the head girl is called—and those of the four house captains, too?"

"I'm not sure that I ought to . . ."

"Love," said Green, as though he had anticipated this protest, "we have the right to search every file, drawer, cupboard or whatever in the school. To confiscate every piece of paper in it. To take the roof off, if necessary. Now you wouldn't want it all to turn that drastic, would you?"

"No. Of course not."

"Five girlies' names then."

"The school captain is also captain of one of the houses."

"O.K. Four names to begin with. Is there a school list in here?"

"Yes."

"Right. Let's see it then."

After the sergeants had left with their information, Masters said: "Now Miss Freeman, those questions."

"Anything I can do to help."

"Thank you. Please sit down. There are chairs for us all."

Miss Freeman settled herself opposite Masters who had taken Miss Holland's chair.

"First off, this study is at the opposite end of the school from the School House . . ."

Miss Freeman didn't let him finish. "Oh, yes. I often said to Miss Holland it was a sabbath day's journey from one to the other."

"How often did you have to make that journey?"

"Quite often."

"More specifically, please. Twice a day? Once a month?"

"Oh, nothing like that. Perhaps once or twice a week."

"For what purposes?"

"For anything that cropped up."

"Isn't this a house phone hanging on the panelling behind the desk?"

"Oh, yes. But it doesn't go to the house. Only to my office and the staff room."

"How would the headmistress get in touch with the three boarding houses?"

"They are too far away for an internal system. Right over on the other side of the school grounds. She had to make an ordinary local call on the GPO phone. But

Miss Holland wasn't one to be always phoning up people. She said that if things were properly organised they would run themselves without a lot of interference from her."

"Are you saying," asked Green, "that she didn't poke her nose in but she knew what was going on?"

"I always said she had a sixth sense because she could always forestall trouble. But all she did, really, was talk to people and listen to what they had to say—both mistresses and girls. There was the business of the tapioca pudding for instance."

"What was that?" asked Masters. "Don't tell me the good old standby of all school cooks has come under fire."

"Just that. Miss Holland would stop girls—boarders —and ask them what they'd had for lunch and whether they'd enjoyed it and eaten it up. It didn't take her long to discover that tapioca was not a favourite and that girls didn't eat it. So Miss Holland just strolled over to the houses and let the cooks and house mistresses know—in a nice sort of way so as not to upset them. She told them that she herself had not been able to stand tapioca and suggested that as it wasn't eaten up they should stop making it. One cook told her it was cheap and they wouldn't be able to afford a substitute. Miss Holland said there was no food as dear as that which wasn't eaten."

"True," said Green. "What did she suggest as fill-belly in its place?"

"We had an old area of ground that was just left to grow wild. Not a big patch, but it was beyond the trees and difficult to get the mowers in. Miss Holland told the groundsman she wanted it cultivating and quick. She suggested potatoes for an immediate crop.

She got them, too. So the houses hadn't to buy them. That was the first year. Now they get all their carrots and onions and lettuce for virtually nothing. Miss Holland wouldn't have exotic things like raspberries grown there, because she said it wouldn't benefit the kitchens with the girls away so long in the summer. But the standard of meals is much higher. She also introduced contract buying. At one time the houses bought things separately. Now they all join together to get bulk prices. It makes quite a difference over the year. Then she cut out broad beans because they weren't popular. She did it in a roundabout way by talking about acquired tastes and how she thought nobody really liked broad beans until they were grown up."

"People got the hint?"

"Yes."

"And she cut costs?"

"Not to save money. She wouldn't have that. Oh, no! To improve things. She got very cross when she discovered one house had saved a lot of money on catering one term. She said the school was not in business to make a profit out of the girls' food fees."

"A very creditable viewpoint. Now, Miss Freeman, tell me why, when Miss Holland was so well organised, you needed to go through to the School House once or twice a week."

"Miss Holland was not in school on Tuesday and Thursday afternoons . . ."

"Games days?"

"Yes. But I was. I worked until five, Mondays to Fridays. So if there were callers or phone calls that I couldn't deal with, I would have to consult her. Mostly I had no need to disturb her. I could usually deal

103

with things myself, or wait until the next day to speak to her. But there are always some things that can't wait, aren't there?"

"Of course. And you couldn't phone her without using the outside phone, so you just popped through to see her."

"Yes."

"Thank you. Now, tell me, what happened when you went through to the School House? Did you knock at the door and wait for it to be answered?"

"No. I'd tap and walk in. Usually I'd see Mrs Gibson, but often I had to find Miss Holland."

"In other words, you were free to come and go?"

"Completely. I'd describe it like being friendly neighbours. You know, where you can pop in the back door and if there's nobody there you coo-ee to draw their attention. That sort of footing."

"That puts it very nicely, Miss Freeman. But it suggests that the house door was always unlocked."

"It was. I never went there when it wasn't."

"Never?"

"Never."

"Not even when you were here in the evenings?"

"I was never in school after normal hours . . . not in the office."

"What exactly does that mean, please?"

"I always come to watch the school play at Christmas. That is always performed on three evenings. And then just before the end of the summer term there's the parents' tennis match. That is in the evening and I come to watch."

"Nothing else?"

"Lots of things, but nothing I come to."

"What?"

"Play rehearsals, orchestra rehearsals, debates and, of course, board meetings. Oh, yes, there's a dance, too, in the hall, at the end of every term."

"Where were the board meetings held?"

"In the library. I showed it to you. Just at the top of the steps outside my office. It's between my room and the junior cloakroom."

"You weren't needed at the meetings?"

"Oh, no. The secretary, Mr Hussey—he's a solicitor —did the minutes. I was never involved in anything so high-powered, except to make sure the caretakers had arranged the room properly—pushed the tables together and set the chairs round. Oh, yes. And to make sure somebody had dusted in there."

"But weren't you needed to take in coffee or to let them in?"

"Nothing like that. The dining-room staff prepared a trolley just before they left. Mrs Gibson usually carried a jug of coffee and one of hot milk through when it was needed."

"I see. She was always present on meeting days?"

"Not always. I have known Miss Holland to ask two of the senior boarders to stand in for Mrs Gibson. I think they used the dining-room kitchen on those occasions."

"I see."

"And as for letting them in . . . Well, that was easy. They came to my door, obviously, and each board member had a key . . ."

"They what?" asked Green.

". . . to the door near my office. Had a key. A Yale. The main gates were left open so that they could park on the concrete. But with the gates open, Miss Holland wouldn't leave the door unlocked, so she gave

each one a key. They let themselves in. It wouldn't
have been right if she had had to go and answer the
door a dozen times herself."

"But so many keys . . . It was unsafe."

"How could it be? Leaving the door unlocked so
that anybody could get in was unsafe. Leaving it
locked so that only authorised people could get in
was much safer."

Green grunted, but said nothing. Masters sat quiet
for a moment and then asked: "Who bore a grudge
against Miss Holland?"

Miss Freeman stared in amazement. "A grudge?
Why, nobody. Miss Holland was not the sort of person
anybody could bear a grudge about. She was just . . .
well, just too fair to cause resentment."

"She's dead," Green reminded her.

"But surely . . ."

"Surely what, love?"

"You're suggesting somebody hated her so much . . ."

"You think she committed suicide?"

"Never."

"Died by accident, then?"

Miss Freeman had no reply. Green went on, after
a pause. "If it was neither suicide nor accident, it was
murder."

"Oh! Yes, I suppose it would be. That's why you're
here, of course. . . ."

"That's right, love. Now, when those two senior
girlies came to make coffee when Mrs Gibson was
away, how did they get into the school?"

"Miss Holland lent them a key, of course. But I
always made sure I got it back next day."

"Whose key? Hers?"

"No, mine. It was a nuisance because I always had
to ring next morning."

Masters asked: "Every member of staff had a key?"

"Not to this door. To the top one. The fourth one up. That's the staff entrance."

"Thank you, Miss Freeman. Now, before we go we'd like to look at the school list. And I think there's a punishment book."

"How did you know that?"

"We know lots, love," said Green.

"The punishment book won't tell you anything. Miss Holland never gave punishments."

"Quite. Most things we look at will tell us nothing, but we have to look, just to make sure."

"Very well, but I don't like this. I shall have to tell Miss Bulmer."

"You do that, love," said Green. "You'd be failing in your duty if you didn't, just as we'd be failing in ours if we didn't look at everything."

Masters took the school list. He glanced down the names. He looked up and said: "I've met the Chairman of the Governors."

"Sir Thomas?"

"Yes. I see there's a Rachel Kenny here. Is that the granddaughter he told me about?"

"Yes. A nice little girl. A bit naughty, perhaps."

"Like all kids. Are there any other children or grandchildren or nieces of governors here, now?"

"Not this year. There were two last year. They both went to Cambridge this term."

"Excellent. Thank you, Miss Freeman. Now the punishment book please."

It was a small, hard-backed ledger. The label on the front said it had been started nearly three years earlier, but there were no more than half a dozen pages filled. Masters glanced through it and then handed it to

107

Green who, after he had finished with it, gave it back to Miss Freeman.

"I told you that wouldn't help you."

"So you did."

"Now," said Masters, "we ought to look into the school business affairs. Just a glance to see there's nothing seriously wrong. I'm sure there isn't, Miss Freeman, but it would be nice to make sure we can say there was no business reason for Miss Holland to take her own life."

"She wouldn't do that."

"I'm certain you're right. But it will be nice to prove everything was in apple-pie order. So, Miss Freeman, we'd better know who the school bursar is—I understand a new one has recently been appointed."

"That is Miss Lickfold."

"Lickfold? Right. Where does she live?"

Miss Freeman told them. Masters' final request was for Miss Freeman to call them a taxi.

When they left the school in the Rover, Reed said: "Back to the nick, mate. I want a street map of this dump, otherwise we're never going to find these addresses."

Masters had told them to interview four girls. Melissa Craig-Deller, school captain and a day girl. Mary Dudson, also a day girl, and two boarders, Elizabeth Milne and Diana Gilbey.

They decided to start at the top with Melissa.

"Double-barrelled name," said Berger as they drew up outside the house, "and double-fronted residence. What our friend Greeny would call a nice pad, don't you think?"

"All gables, white paint and good curtains. Daddy

must have a bit of money. I reckon the Chief would do better than us at this place."

"He sent us."

"So he did. Come on."

It was Mrs Craig-Deller who answered the door and invited them in as soon as she learned their identities and before they had stated their business. Both men were impressed. She was young—Reed guessed less than forty—jolly, and personable. She led them into a chintzy sitting room with a good deal of exquisite glass dotted about—paperweights, candlesticks and vases.

"It's your daughter, Miss Melissa, we have come to speak to, ma'am."

"I guessed it was. I'll get her for you. She's up in the playroom with two friends—Mary Dudson and her brother Charles. Mary and Melissa are great friends." She smiled. "So are Charles and Melissa. Young love, you know. He's down from university on some sort of reading week which I confess I regard as a complete skive as they've not been up more than about three weeks this term. However . . ."

"We would like to see Miss Dudson, too."

"You've struck lucky then. But may I ask why, specifically? I realise you must be here to make inquiries into Miss Holland's death . . ."

"Quite right, ma'am. No specific reason really. We are, in effect, just asking general questions. Our Chief, Superintendent Masters, works that way. He likes to get the background picture. There's no reason why you shouldn't be present when we talk to the young ladies."

"Thank you. I was going to suggest that. Now, just give me a minute. I'll have to toil right upstairs to warn them. They won't hear a shout—not above the noise of pop music."

109

Berger said: "Would it be easier if we went up there? What I mean is, ma'am, we don't want a formal meeting. We shan't be taking anything down in writing. It's just a chat we want."

She smiled. "If you don't mind squatting on a bean-bag, it would be a good idea. I tell you what, I'll ask Mrs Parker—she's my daily—to make us some coffee."

"If it's not too much trouble . . ."

"It will add to your informal atmosphere. I'd rather not subject the young to too serious a session with the police myself. And that lot up there would drink coffee till the cows came home. They have this horrible habit of referring to it as 'a coffee'. Have 'a coffee'! Why the indefinite article the whole time I don't know. It probably has something to do with those ghastly mugs they drink it from. I suppose one could call those indefinite articles, couldn't one?"

Reed grinned. "You ought to meet our Chief, ma'am. He'd like your style."

She blushed slightly. "Am I running on a bit? I expect I'm a bit nervous at meeting real detectives for the first time in my life."

"We're quite harmless, ma'am."

"Are you? Really? My husband heard last night that Superintendent Masters had arrived and he told me he is far from harmless. William said he was a scourge."

"So he is—of criminals, ma'am. But a more ordinary decent bloke would be hard to find. And he's got a smashing wife."

"I see. Come along, then."

She left them standing at the foot of the close-carpeted stairs while she arranged for coffee to be sent up, then she went ahead of them. The playroom was an attic room with sloping ceilings and only five-foot

110

walls. The three occupants looked round as the three visitors entered. Melissa, curled up on what was obviously a single divan covered in a travelling rug, sat up and reached to turn off the record player which was belting out a million decibels of pop.

"Mummy?"

"I've brought two detectives from Scotland Yard to see you."

As the sergeants moved into the room, the three young people all got silently to their feet.

"I'm Sergeant Reed and this is Sergeant Berger. Please sit down again. All we want is to chat to you for a few minutes."

"It's about Miss Holland, isn't it?" asked Melissa.

"Poor old Dutch," said Mary Dudson.

"You are genuinely sorry about her death?" asked Berger as they all looked round to see where best to sit. It was a bit of a problem. The divan took Melissa and her mother. Two armchairs—obviously discarded from other rooms in the house—were offered to the sergeants by Charles Dudson, while he and his sister prepared to squat, apparently quite happily, on a giant cushion. The room was almost completely papered—ceilings and all—with large, colourful posters. There were heaps of books, a table with all sorts of oddments on it—from tennis rackets to coloured chalks—and several large record-carriers looking like squared-up briefcases.

"Sorry? I should just think we are. Everyone is. Lord knows who we'll get in her place. Nobody half as good, that's for sure."

"Good?" asked Reed.

"They mean decent," said Charles Dudson, in a man-to-man tone. "Understanding, I suppose. At least I thought so. And not stuffy."

111

"You knew her, too, sir?"

"And how!" said his sister. "He fell for her in a big way, didn't he, Mel? After last year's Christmas dance. We didn't get anything out of him for days except Miss Holland this and Miss Holland that. It nearly drove Mummy up the wall."

"Rubbish," said Charles loftily. "I just appreciated what a fine woman she was."

"With a smasher like Mel around? You went all soulful for at least a week. Daddy had to tell you about it. I heard him. On Christmas Eve. He said he didn't mind you falling for an older woman but he was damned if he was going to have her as the spectre at the family feast."

Mrs Craig-Deller laughed, and Melissa said: "That's right, Chas. I couldn't get a word out of you. I didn't even get a kiss under the mistletoe."

"He's made up for it since, haven't you, Chas?" said his sister, poking him in the ribs.

"Look," said the aggrieved young male. "You invited me to your school dance and I came. To my great surprise I saw your headmistress, whom I'd never met before, getting up for every dance. Not just for the waltzes and things, but for the disco numbers, too. Now that was something, you must admit. But she looked great, too."

"Not bad," admitted Mary. "She dressed well."

"I was impressed by that alone," said Charles. "But then she asked me to dance with her. And I got another surprise. Called me Mr Dudson and told me that while she did not disapprove of my friendship with Mel she did disapprove of my occupying so much of her time that her schoolwork was suffering, and she would be delighted if I could see my way clear not to spoil the academic prospects of one of the most charming and promising of her senior pupils."

"You never told me," accused Melissa.

"Didn't want to give you a big head. But I promised to do what I could and just because I tried not to interfere with your work too much you all thought I'd deserted you for her." He shook his head in mock sorrow. "It's a hard life for decent chaps like me."

"Pull the other one," said his sister, changing her position on the bean-bag.

At that moment Mrs Parker entered with a shopping basket in one hand, and a large percolator in the other. "This was the best way I could think of to get this lot up here," she said with a laugh. "Here you are. A basket full of cups and saucers and a bottle of milk. There's a jug in there too, Mrs Craig-Deller, so don't let them use it from the bottle, because that's what they will do if you don't watch them."

"Thank you, Mrs Parker."

While their hostess and her daughter sorted out the coffee, Charles asked: "I say, are you getting what you came for? I mean, all this chat about things—that isn't the way the Yard works, is it?"

"We're doing well enough," said Reed. "What you've got to appreciate is that we don't know anything about Miss Holland, who was a very familiar figure to most of you. Now you all tell us she was well liked. We didn't know that. It could have been that everybody hated her guts. So, if somebody killed her, that person will be the odd one out and not one of a vast crowd. My boss always says it's easier to find a needle in a haystack than pick out one particular needle from a heap of needles as big as a haystack."

"I suppose so."

"Particularly if you've armed yourself with a magnet."

"Quite."

"Your coffee, Mr Reed," said Melissa, handing it to him.

"Thank you." As she sat down again, he said: "You're the school captain. Senior girl, in fact, so you must know something of what goes on. You've told us that all the girls liked Miss Holland, but what about the mistresses? Did they all like her?"

Melissa and Mary exchanged glances.

"Please tell me if you know something."

"Miss Lickfold."

"What about her?"

"The Old Dutch beat her to it, didn't she? Lickspit was senior mistress before the Old Dutch came, and expected to be appointed headmistress. She didn't like it when she wasn't."

"Had she good reason to be disappointed?"

"Lickspit? None at all. She's the world's worst teacher. The original haemorrhoid."

"Melissa!" Her mother sounded scandalised.

"You know she's a pain in the neck, Mummy. You've always said she was, even when she taught *you*."

"Please don't refer to her as you did."

"As a haemorrhoid?" asked Mary innocently. "It's only the name of a serpent, after all. A hideous serpent whose bite was said to cause bleeding that could not be stopped . . . what's the word? . . . Unstaunchable, that's it."

"I'm like you," Charles said to Reed. "I'm learning things, even from the young of the species."

"Let's try and work this out, Miss Melissa," said Reed. "Miss Lickfold resented Miss Holland being appointed over her. But now Miss Lickfold is, presumably, again in the running for the post—as senior assistant mistress."

"Not this time. The Old Dutch put her out to grass. She's the new bursar, and Miss Bulmer is deputy headmistress."

"Ah!"

"What does that mean?" asked Charles.

"Work it out for yourself," retorted Reed. "It makes Miss Bulmer's motive as big as Miss Lickfold's."

Charles stared for a moment. "By jove, so it does. One heartbeat from the presidency, so to speak. So now you've got two of the staff as suspects. I'm beginning to see how you chaps work."

Mrs Craig-Deller said: "I don't think we should talk about suspects, Chas. I don't like it."

"Suspects for what?" asked Melissa.

"Be your age," said Charles. "Why do you think half Scotland Yard is in Bramthorpe, with whizz-kid Masters marching on before? Because somebody's been found parking on a double-yellow traffic warden?"

"Oh!"

"Hanky-panky, dearie," said Mary. "The Old Dutch was as healthy as a row of prize cabbages and she wasn't the sort to make a mistake over a heap of laburnum seeds, now was she?"

"I suppose not." Melissa turned to Reed. "It's all rather dreadful, isn't it?"

"I'm afraid so, Miss."

"When Miss Bulmer told the school Miss Holland had died—and we all thought she'd died quite naturally of a heart attack or something—everybody was sad. Some even cried. I said so to Miss Bulmer, and she told me that from the platform she had seen a definite sense of shock on several girls' faces."

The mood of the gathering had changed suddenly. It was quieter.

"A lot of girls?" asked Berger.

"Miss Bulmer didn't say, exactly, but my impression was that she meant just two or three. Several. Yes. I remember now. She said several."

"So you speak for the whole school when you say she was liked and will be missed?"

"I certainly think so."

"Thank you," said Reed. "I don't think we need take up any more of your time except . . ."

"Except what?" asked Charles.

"I was going to ask the young ladies if they had heard any rumours concerning Miss Holland."

"Rumours?" asked Mary. "What sort of rumours?"

"Any sort," replied Reed. "I'm not saying there were any. We haven't heard any. But if there were . . . Well, sometimes there's a basis of truth in rumours."

"What sort of rumour?" Mary asked again.

"Any sort. That she was to lead the next Everest expedition or become a professor somewhere or even to enter a nunnery. As I say, I know of none. I'm simply asking if there were any."

"Not a breath," replied Melissa. "No scandal, no rumours, no murky past, no hectic future."

"Thank you. That closes one door so that we don't have to go haring off on some wild goose chase." He got to his feet. "Thank you all, once again. You've been very helpful."

"Were they helpful?" asked Mrs Craig-Deller as she escorted them downstairs.

"I think so, ma'am. At least we're beginning to get a picture of Miss Holland. That always helps."

She smiled and showed them out.

"Back to the boarding houses," said Berger. "I wonder if we'll get any joy there."

Reed pursed his lips. "It all depends what you mean by joy. Those two were sitting there showing enough thigh to make a man's eyes pop out. If you call that joy, we got a lot of it."

"Nice, though, wasn't it?" said Berger appreciatively. "Uninhibited, these public-school girls, these days. What I liked about it . . ."

"I know what you liked about it."

"Listen. They weren't doing it for effect or for our benefit or anything like that. It was natural—innocent if you like. I suppose they always sprawl about like that and think nothing of it."

"I wouldn't know. Do we turn left here, or keep straight on?"

"Left."

Berger, using the road map, guided Reed to a road parallel to the hill on which the main school building stood and more than a quarter of a mile behind it. Here stood the three boarding houses, separated by the playing fields from the College itself. They were big, square, red-brick edifices, flat sided, each side seemingly full of sash windows all the same size. A common wall topped by railings and backed by a hedge stood in front of them, but there were no dividing walls. They rose from an apron of brownish-yellow gravel which appeared to be seldom used.

"There'll be doors at the back of these places that the kids use to go to and from school," said Berger.

"That's about the size of it." Reed drew in opposite the high wrought-iron gate. "I'll leave the car here. No point in scrunching over that lot."

"Hold hard. I'd better get this sorted. There's one

117

called Milne, and she's in Camfield House, and the other is Gilbey, and she's in Groombridge House. The only problem is, which is which?"

"There's only one way to find out." Reed got out and locked his door. "We're opposite the middle one, so we'll go there. What's the betting it's not one of the ones we want?"

He was wrong. Unreadable from the road was a small modern name-plate, white lettering sunk in brown metal, and measuring no more than six inches by two. It carried the one word "Groombridge". Reed rang the bell.

A young woman answered the door. She wore a twin-set and a tweed skirt in heather mixture. She had blonde, short-cut hair and was so athletically built that Reed immediately catalogued her mentally as the hockey mistress.

"You'll be the detectives," she said before the two men could announce themselves. "Miss Freeman rang to tell us you would be coming. Miss Groombridge and Miss Camfield are both here with the two prefects you wish to see—Elizabeth Milne and Diana Gilbey."

"Thank you. May we come in?"

"Yes, of course. Sorry. I'm the junior mistress in Groombridge. I was detailed to watch out for you." She closed the door behind them. It was a large hall with a polished floor and a square of Turkey carpet. A wide staircase rose from one side. There were white doors opening off the hall and a glass-fronted wall case containing keys, each with a white, pear-shaped tag, hanging on numbered hooks.

"Miss Groombridge's study is here, on the right."

They were led into a room which surprised and pleased Reed. Apart from the big desk in the window it had an old suite, with two huge wing-backed chairs and a three-seater settee in a figured grey-blue velvet with vast cushions, an upright piano with brass candle-holders, a long-pile carpet in faded sweet-pea colours and a log fire burning in a grate which had vertical polished copper reflector-plates on both sides. The fireplace itself was old-fashioned white marble, with a deep fender also in copper, and a thick, wide mantelpiece with a pendulum clock and several little silver photograph frames. To Reed it was lovely, inviting, comfortable, cosy . . .

And so was Miss Groombridge. Though unmarried and living and working her whole time in a female community, she must have come from a family with men in it—brothers as well as father. She knew how to treat these—to her—young men. She struck the right note: no heartiness, no coyness.

"As the girls you wish to interview are pupils, Miss Camfield and I feel we have a duty to be present at your meeting." She turned to the woman occupying one of the armchairs. "This is Miss Camfield. You have already met Miss Fryer. None of us knows much about police procedure, but we feel we must insist on being here."

Reed replied: "As you say, it is your duty to be here, and Sergeant Berger and I would not wish to speak to the two young ladies except in your presence."

"Excellent."

"Before the girls join us, I would like to assure you that neither they, nor any of you ladies, are under any form of suspicion."

"I should hope not. But it's nice to hear you say it."

Miss Camfield asked: "What is the object of your visit, then? And why Elizabeth Milne and Diana Gilbey?"

"Detective Superintendent Masters picked four

119

names at random from the school list. He confined himself to prefects because he had no desire to involve junior girls in any way. He and Inspector Green are talking to various mistresses, the housekeeper and the school secretary. We are doing it simply to get background information. You will appreciate that four men who come new into a town like Bramthorpe, with no knowledge of the person whose death they have come to investigate, are at a loss to know where to start if there are no obvious material clues to help them. The one person we know to have been involved is Miss Holland herself. All we can do is to concentrate on her—her friends, colleagues and contacts. Was she liked? Hated? Mistrusted? Was her way of life such as to breed enemies? If she was universally liked, we know the field of those who wished her harm will be small. If she was disliked the field could be vast. We have to decide these matters as soon as possible. In a school such as this, we have a unique opportunity to assess the character of the late headmistress because there are hundreds of articulate people with whom she was in daily contact. Yourselves, the pupils and the non-academic staff. Each group will have viewed her from a different standpoint: professional colleague, mentor or employer. And as experience has taught us that very often the character of the victim of homicide has some bearing on the crime, we are anxious to learn all we can of Miss Holland's character."

"Sergeant," said Miss Groombridge, "that was an edifying explanation. But we've kept you standing all this time. Please sit down."

"Leave the sofa for the girls," suggested Berger. "We don't want them to be anything but comfortable. This is only a chat, after all. I'll take the piano stool, and Sergeant Reed can have your desk chair."

"No sitting with the light playing on faces or anything of that sort?" asked Miss Fryer.

"No, ma'am. And no notes, either."

"Good," said Miss Groombridge. "Now, if there are no more questions, we can have the girls in." She turned to Miss Fryer. "Margaret, call them, please, and bring the tea trolley, too. I'm sure the sergeants could do with a cup. I know I could."

It took a few minutes for everybody to get settled and served with tea and scones. Although Reed and Berger, fresh from coffee with Mrs Craig-Deller, had no need of the tea, by unspoken but mutual consent they did not refuse.

Reed put his untouched cup of tea on the desk. "Miss Groombridge, I shall put my questions to the two prefects, and while it is their opinions we are seeking, we don't want to exclude you three ladies. So, please, put in your penn'orth if you wish—any of you."

"Thank you."

"Miss Milne, was Miss Holland a kind person?"

"Oh, yes. Very kind."

"You have had personal experience of little kindnesses from her?"

"No . . o . . o. I don't think so. Not exactly." Elizabeth Milne wore spectacles. She was, in Reed's view, no beauty, but she had glorious hair, so dark as to be nearly black. Shoulder length and exceedingly well cut, it shone in the light from the fire and the two reading lamps Miss Groombridge had switched on.

"You base your opinion on kindnesses to other girls?"

Elizabeth looked at Diana Gilbey, who shrugged. "No," she replied.

"Did she mark your work leniently, for instance?"

"Never," exclaimed Diana, who was a podgy, jolly-looking fair girl with a snub nose. "Not likely. She was down on us like a ton of bricks if we made a mistake or for untidy work."

"Lenient over punishments, perhaps?"

"She never needed to give punishments. You could hear a pin drop in her periods—even before she got to the form room door."

"Strict disciplinarian, was she?"

Again the two girls exchanged glances. "Well," said Elizabeth, "she was and she wasn't."

"Please explain."

"I don't think I can. I've never thought about it, because the question never occurred to me." She turned to Miss Groombridge. "There was no reason why it should. The good behaviour just happened because everybody knew that's what the staff expected."

"Quite right, Elizabeth." The housemistress turned to Reed. "Young people sometimes rebel against discipline, but they like it there, in the background, just the same. They then know exactly where they are. It provides guidelines. Excuses even."

"Excuses?"

"If somebody is urging them to do something they know is wrong and don't wish to do—something, say, as simple as staying out too late—they can always say they can't do whatever it is and blame it on to their parents or headmistress or whoever has laid down the rules."

"I see." Reed turned to the girls. "So can I take it then that Miss Holland engendered a feeling of kindness not by soppiness, but by imposing a strict, fair discipline which girls could appreciate because it was never unjust or unreasonable?"

"That's it. That's just it," said Diana. "She was reliable."

"Thank you. So would you say all the girls liked her? Most of them? Or just some of them?"

"Everybody," said both girls together.

Reed smiled. "There seems to be no doubt about that. So, when the girls knew Miss Holland was dead, what was their reaction?"

"I don't understand?"

"Did they spend their time wondering who the new headmistress would be? Did they cry? Were they sad? Were they shocked?"

"It was terrible," said Elizabeth quietly. "At first, that was. I was standing at the end of the form I'm responsible for—that's the Upper Fourth—and I thought we were going to have a few fainting fits."

"Why?"

"Some—one or two—went so white."

"Shock?"

"I suppose so."

Reed turned to Miss Groombridge. "You were on the platform, ma'am? Did you see signs of shock?"

"Not specifically shock, but every emotion from dismay to sadness."

"Miss Camfield?"

"I'm trying to remember exactly my thoughts at the time. I'm sure I said to myself that the effect of the news was so great that some of them were even frightened. Understandable, of course. Sudden death takes people in different ways, and there were three hundred young people down there in the hall, some of whom are really very young."

"Thank you. Miss Fryer?"

"I remember thinking that one girl was going to faint and I'd have to go down to her. I do the first aid, you know."

"Your services were not required?"

"No. The girls on either side of her seemed to rally her."

"How?"

"I remember they spoke to her pretty urgently, and one took her arm. She pulled herself together then."

"Why should she faint, do you think?"

"She didn't actually faint."

"Why should she look as though she were about to?"

Miss Fryer reddened slightly, but Miss Groombridge answered quite matter-of-factly. "This is a girls' school, Sergeant Reed. Faints are not uncommon among young girls at the time of puberty. We must average two or three a term perhaps. Some of the girls of that age have a trying time and any sudden stress or shock just at the wrong moment will cause a faint."

"I see."

"The horrors can be a damn nuisance when they first start," agreed Diana Gilbey without turning a hair.

"I see." Reed turned to Berger, who looked up at him—having been very absorbed in the pattern on the carpet during this last exchange. Berger said: "So nothing out of the ordinary happened, you might say."

"Nothing whatsoever."

"We'll leave that then." Berger turned to Miss Groombridge. "I don't want to tread on any toes here, so please don't answer if you'd rather not. But you will appreciate that in a case like this we have to ask questions about who is likely to benefit, or who might bear a grudge."

"The girls have told you nobody bore Miss Holland a grudge."

"So they have. But her appointment here must have disappointed somebody."

"Lickers," said Elizabeth promptly.

"Please ignore that," said Miss Groombridge.

"You mean Miss Lickfold was not disappointed at the time?"

"You know Miss Lickfold applied for the post?"

"Yes."

"Then why ask us to comment if you know about it?"

"I did say you weren't to answer if you preferred not to."

"I say," interjected Diana Gilbey, "you'd better answer, Miss Groombridge. Detectives always say you leave them free to form their own conclusions if you don't."

Reed laughed. "I suspect you're more interested in the reply than we would be." He turned to Miss Groombridge. "We'll go no further along that line in mixed company, ma'am. In fact, we'll finish there, I think."

"I would prefer, nevertheless, to state that Miss Lickfold, though disappointed at the time, has had more than three years to get over that disappointment and that she is, in any case, a gentle soul."

Reed paused a moment before replying. Then—

"We have heard different, ma'am. Not everybody agrees that she is gentle."

"The girls wouldn't," said Elizabeth Milne decisively. "She abused her power."

"I think," said Miss Groombridge wryly, "that I will accept your offer to end this conversation, Sergeant."

"Yes, ma'am. But it does demonstrate to you very clearly how often the opinions we hear vary to such a degree that at times they are diametrically opposed."

* * *

Miss Lickfold lived in a semi-detached house in Stratford Avenue. The house was of the front, middle and back variety, with no garage. A side passage alone separated it from its neighbour and led to the back door. This side passage had a gate, still bearing an old plate with the legend "Tradesmen", and another saying "No Hawkers no Circulars".

"This is going back a bit," said Green. "When was it built? About 1920?"

"I imagine so. It was probably an avenue in those days. There are still a few trees, but it's almost a main road now."

Their knock was answered by Miss Lickfold herself. As Masters knew, she was nearing retirement age, but he hadn't expected to see so drab a person, from whom all vitality seemed to have ebbed.

"No doubt Miss Freeman rang to say we were on our way. We are from Scotland Yard."

"Miss Freeman did warn me."

"May we come in and talk to you?"

"Of course. Please follow me."

She was dressed in a suit of indeterminate colour. A mixture of grey and plum was how Masters noted it privately. She had a brown sweater under the jacket and a heavy string of beads. Her hair was short, straight and grey, and she wore rimless spectacles.

Miss Lickfold led them to the middle room. The house smelt stuffy, as though the air was never changed but mixed with the smell of medicaments and ripe fruit.

"I understand your mother is an invalid, Miss Lickfold. I hope we shall not disturb her."

"She has her bed in the front room. She will have seen or heard your arrival, so I'll just pop in to tell her who you are, otherwise she will be calling for information. Her life is so uneventful she has become very inquisitive."

"Quite right, too," said Green. "You go and tell her we've called for a chat. We can wait a minute."

"Thank you. Please sit down."

It was a shabby room, but strangely comfortable. The window looked out over a patch of concrete yard which ran up to the garden grass. The room itself was evidently Miss Lickfold's utility room. It had a dining table which she obviously used as a desk and from which, Masters guessed, she ate her lonely meals. There were two old hide chairs, one on each side of the fireplace, four dining chairs and an art nouveau sideboard littered with all manner of items—books, gloves, a scarf, an empty decanter and a cut-glass jug, a purse and several other packages.

"I like this," said Green. "We had one just like it when I was a kid. We used to eat in the kitchen and live in this one. We had one of the wireless sets in the windows with accumulators on the floor . . ."

He got no further. Miss Lickfold rejoined them. Green ushered her to one of the armchairs. He and Masters took dining chairs.

Masters began.

"You have probably heard, Miss Lickfold, that an open verdict was returned at the inquest on Miss Holland this morning."

"I heard before I left the school."

"It means that we have to try to determine exactly how she came to take the laburnum seeds which killed her."

"I cannot see, Superintendent, how I can possibly help you."

"Perhaps not, ma'am, but we must ask a lot of questions in the hope that somebody will be able to give us a hint or two. You, I understand, are the new bursar of the school."

"I took up the post in September."

"Having been a teacher at the school for many years?"

"I was deputy headmistress for almost nine of those years."

"Then you, obviously, must know more than most about the school itself and, since you were her deputy, about Miss Holland, too."

"Despite our respective positions, we were never close."

"Why was that?"

"Miss Holland and I were of different generations."

"But, allowing for the difference in your ages, was there any other reason for your not working closely?"

"Many reasons. As you may already know, I considered that after many years as deputy headmistress, I should have been appointed to the headship when that post fell vacant. Miss Holland was brought in over my head."

"Naturally you resented that."

"Intensely. And not only because I considered my experience at Bramthorpe qualified me for the job, but also because the bigger salary and the provision of the School House would have meant so much to me and to my mother."

Green asked: "But that disappointment would have been there if somebody other than Miss Holland had been given the job in preference to you?"

"Quite."

"So the resentment was not directed at Miss Holland personally, but at the person who superseded you?" asked Masters.

"I'm afraid you cannot split hairs like that. Miss

Holland was there, in person. I could not direct my resentment against an impersonal shadow."

"I understand. But after Miss Holland's arrival, what then? Was she an ogre?"

"To me, personally? Yes."

"Personally, or professionally?"

"I suppose I mean the latter. I can recall no actual personal unkindness, but after so long my personal and professional lives have fused together. What affects the one affects the other, and vice versa."

"So she slighted you, professionally?"

"Unforgivably."

"So you still feel the resentment, even though you are no longer teaching?"

"Undeniably."

"We'd better hear a few of the details," said Green.

"Why?"

"Look, Miss Lickfold, if Miss Holland was the type to ride roughshod over an able, experienced and loyal teacher like you, she probably treated scores of other people in the same way. That means she'd not be short of enemies. What you tell us may help to identify them."

"I see. But I have no wish to go into details."

"That's a pity, but probably the other mistresses will tell us how disgracefully you were treated."

"No, they won't," she replied bitterly. "They all fell into line with all her new-fangled ideas. Miss Holland turned Bramthorpe into nothing more than an examination factory. I was the only one . . ."

"The only one what?"

"Everything I did was wrong in her eyes. My disciplinary measures, the work I set, everything. She thought, because she was M.A., Oxon. and B.Sc., London, that she knew all there was to know about every subject. But there was one subject she knew nothing about, and that was bringing up young people. She thought good examination results were everything. Education should teach girls to be dutiful and obedient even if their passes in external examinations are a grade or two lower. Our girls were sent to us to be taught to be young ladies, not future protestors."

Masters nodded. "I think I see your point. So how did Miss Holland slight you?"

"She stopped me teaching in the upper school."

"That could have been in order to strengthen the teaching in the lower school."

"I hardly think so, in view of the fact that she then manoeuvred me out of teaching altogether."

"To become bursar?"

"Yes."

"You don't like the post?"

"I'm a teacher."

"Yet you agreed to become bursar. Why, in view of the fact that you could not be dismissed from your teaching job?"

"There are more ways than one of skinning a cat. I could not be dismissed from the school, but I could have the position of deputy headmistress taken from me."

"Miss Holland threatened to do that?"

"I was told that whether I accepted the post of bursar or not, Miss Bulmer, the senior maths mistress, would be appointed deputy headmistress at the beginning of this term."

"An ultimatum, in fact?"

"Just so."

"But was there no quid pro quo?"

"How do you mean?"

"Wasn't it Miss Holland's intention to allow you to

130

carry on as bursar for an extra five years, thereby not only allowing you to continue on full salary but also offering the prospect of an increased pension at the end of your service?"

Miss Lickfold didn't answer for a moment. Then—

"Yes, damn her, that was her scheme. Offering me charity because she knew I couldn't afford to refuse it. Just to further her own ends . . ."

"Steady, love," said Green. "Don't get worked up about it. She's dead now."

"Yes, she is. And I'm glad. Very glad. I don't care how she died. She deserved it."

Masters looked across at Green and gestured towards the door. They got up quietly and left the house.

CHAPTER V

They met once more in Masters' room. The sergeants had had the foresight to bring in a stock of beer.

"We've got just seventy-two minutes before dinner," said Masters. "I want to hear what you two have heard, and the D.C.I. will tell you what we learned. Then I want to get down there to eat as soon as the dining room opens because I think we may have to go out again."

"You've got something in mind, George?"

"Yes. I'll discuss it over dinner. Reports now."

Reed and Berger spoke first. Masters and Green listened attentively. When they had finished, Green spoke.

"Are you going to take the Lickfold woman in for questioning, Chief?" asked Berger.

"I don't think so. Certainly not at the moment."

"From the way the D.C.I. spoke, she practically confessed."

"I'm sure he didn't mean to imply that."

"No," said Green. "The woman needs treatment. She's caved in, mentally, under the stress of her home life and the severe blows to her self-esteem dealt by Miss Holland."

"But from everything we've heard, Miss Holland was a decent, kind woman."

"Besides being kind, she was efficient and devoted," Masters reminded him. "Efficiency and devotion are uncomfortable traits in a headmistress because, though Miss Holland was a kindly woman, she was not prepared to accept the too obvious shortcomings of Miss Lickfold. Devotion to her job led her to harry the weak member of the team even though, in doing so, she made better provision for that member than Miss Lickfold had any right to expect. Wounds to the self-esteem, it would seem, are not cured by kindness, only by restoratives—literally—which . . . well, which restore the injured party to the former state of self-regard."

"Is that why you didn't collect her?"

"That's it," said Green. "We could be wrong, so we shan't forget her, but we were both of the opinion she had lost some of her marbles. To have taken her in, without very strong cause, could have been a big mistake. There's her mother to be looked after, for instance. Apart from the fact that neither of us thought she was guilty. I mean, she wasn't cunning. She took no trouble to disguise her dislike of Miss Holland. We were left with just a picture of frustration and hatred. But as I say, we could be wrong."

"And there was nothing else?"

"Not then, but there is now. His Nibs has got some bee in his bonnet from all the signs."

"Is that right, Chief?"

"It's certainly been strengthened during the last half hour."

"What has?"

"An idea which you gave me earlier."

"Me?" asked Reed, in amazement.

"Yes. Something you said to Berger last night. So drink up and we'll go and get something to eat. Don't forget the D.C.I. and myself were not provided with tea and cake everywhere we went this afternoon."

"The food's not bad here," said Green, tackling a plate of beef stew with noodles, "but there's not enough of it. I like a pub that lets you have a decent helping and then some more. If we're going out again tonight I shall look for a Chinese chippy. Something to go with the beer before we go to bed."

"We are going out," said Masters.

"All together?"

"Yes. The School House first."

"Going to put Mrs Gibson through the hoop?"

"Not Mrs Gibson. The house itself."

Green finished his beef and picked up the menu. "Coupe Jacques," he said. "I have my suspicions about that. I'll go for the rhubarb tart."

"It means a dollop of ice cream with half a tinned peach on it."

"Is that so? I wouldn't want it then."

"You don't like ice cream?"

"I don't like simple things tarted up with names like that." He turned to Masters. "Mrs Gibson will think we've come to give her the Coupe Jacques if we arrive without warning."

"I'd rather arrive unannounced."

"Suit yourself."

"You have some serious objection?"

"Nothing that would seem important to you, perhaps. But it can't be funny for a woman alone in a house where there's just been a death to have four dirty great jacks descend upon her after dark, without warning."

Masters considered this for a moment and then said: "Right. I'll bow to your wishes. Two of us will go.

Berger will be one of them, because she knows him. As to the other, it will be either yourself or Reed."

"Why the choice? And why not you, personally?"

"I've got several visits in mind. I'll do one of the other calls. You can come with me or go with Berger."

Green grunted his thanks as the helping of rhubarb tart was put in front of him. Then looking up at the waitress, he asked: "Have you got a lemon, love?"

"A lemon, sir?"

"Yes. I'm looking for an answer, you see."

The bewildered girl moved away from him as if not quite sure of his mental stability. Masters said: "Please don't worry. That was one of the Chief Inspector's jokes. What he'd really like is the cheeseboard as soon as he's finished his rhubarb tart."

When the girl had gone, Green turned to Masters. "What decision would you make if you were me?"

"I'd come with me. After the call I hope to make I'll join Berger and whoever his companion is at the School House. Coming with us you'd get it both ways."

"I'll forgo the biscuits and cheese."

"Please don't. I want to make a phone call before I leave."

"What are Sergeant Reed and I to do when we get to the School House, Chief?"

"Wait for me. Chat up Mrs Gibson, and don't let her into the kitchen. So refuse tea or coffee if she offers it to you."

"Right, Chief. But I must say it sounds a rum assignment."

Reed and Berger had taken a taxi. Masters was driving the Rover.

"Would you mind telling me what we're about?" asked Green.

"I thought you'd like to meet Sir Thomas Kenny."

"Why him? You saw him last night."

"Tonight we are to meet his son and daughter-in-law."

Green sat silent for a minute or two. Then he said: "I'm growing more like the sergeants every day. I'm getting to the stage where I'm beginning to think that everything you do must have some reasonable purpose behind it. So I'll accept that you've manufactured this meeting for a good reason. But I don't know what it is. Are you going to tell me?"

"Yes. At least, I want to tell you my idea, and then you can laugh, scoff, sneer or even agree that it has possibilities."

"I'm listening."

Masters spoke as he drove. When he had finished, Green said: "All I'm saying at the moment is that it fits where it touches."

"No outright condemnation?"

"No. But I'd want some more datum points before I'd go solid on it."

"But you agree it is worth following up?"

"You'll have to see Miss Bulmer, the hockey mistress, and probably Miss Freeman again."

"Agreed. And the kitchen."

"That above all. So cut this chat short, George, and let's get over there pronto."

Sir Thomas himself let them in. "Norman and Barbara are here and are wondering why you wish to see them."

"You told them it was just general background I was after, Sir Thomas?"

"Yes. This is Mr Green, isn't it? I saw you in the courtroom, Chief Inspector."

The two shook hands. "Masters did a good job this morning, getting Gilchrist to give an open verdict, don't you think?"

"He's got the gift of the gab," admitted Green. "But he did well enough."

"Were we right to ask for you?"

"If you mean have we turned up anything to justify our intervention, it is a bit early to say for sure, but the signs are that you were right."

"I'm pleased to hear it. Come in and meet my family."

Norman Kenny was not in the least like his father. He was a biggish man, and at forty was running slightly to fat. He was also balding. His wife, Barbara, was a small, sharp-featured woman, with expensively coiffured hair and rimless glasses with a silver chain attached to the ear pieces. She wore long, dangling amethyst earrings so that every movement of her head created a disturbance. Her nose was slightly hooked and her lips thin. Masters put her down as a shrew, and had serious doubts as to whether Sir Thomas would like her very much.

Norman was dull. He had none of the sparkle of his father and was even hesitant in his speech. When he was introduced to the two detectives, he sounded grumpy. Masters wondered about it. Was it just a mannerism, or had he adopted this after years of marriage to Barbara?

"Mr Masters and Mr Green believe they already have reasons to suggest that Mabel did not die a natural death."

"Really!" said Barbara. "I personally think it best to let sleeping dogs lie."

"Gr-r-umph," said Norman. "Muck-raking. Could cause a lot of grief."

"To whom?" asked Masters blandly. "Have you anybody particularly in mind?"

"Father, for one."

"Sir Thomas was responsible for having us brought here."

"That was a mistake," said Barbara dogmatically. "If he had consulted us first, we'd have dissuaded him."

"Rubbish," growled Sir Thomas. "Since when has anybody dissuaded me from doing anything I'd set my mind on?"

"Nevertheless, Father, I think you will regret it," said his daughter-in-law."

"May I ask you why you say that, ma'am?" asked Masters.

"Certainly. The local police, I understand, were satisfied. They know Bramthorpe and its people. Why not let them do their job? Your arrival has started all sorts of rumours, all of them, no doubt, false. They succeeded only in upsetting a community which is as law-abiding as anywhere in the country. That can do nothing but harm. And to what purpose? It may well be that you will find nothing and so all the stir will have been pointless."

"There's a lot in what you say," said Green, surprisingly. "It's an argument we hear often in our business. Usually from people who scream loudest once the lid has blown. What I mean is, ma'am, what would you say if another prominent citizen were to die tonight in similar circumstances, and another next week? Wouldn't you say the police should have done something at the outset?"

"A specious argument. This is not the East End of London."

"I think we'll all have a drink," said Sir Thomas. "Norman, do the honours." He turned to Masters. "I should have told you that Norman is managing director of my group. I'm the chairman. Barbara's father was a baker—in a big way, of course. His goods were packaged and sold all over the south. He made lemonade, too. I can remember his dandelion and burdock, years ago, and American ice-cream soda. In bottles with glass marbles at the top for stoppers."

Masters was watching Barbara Kenny. He got the impression she didn't altogether like hearing her father referred to as a baker.

"Penny monsters?" asked Green. "I always went for cherryade. It tasted the same as the others, but I liked the colour."

Norman handed his wife a glass of sherry and to the men he gave whisky. "What," he grumped to Masters, "did you want to see us about?"

"It's delicate," replied Masters, including Sir Thomas in the reply.

"In what way?"

"I was proceeding on the assumption that your engagement to Miss Holland was a secret known only to the three of you here in this room. Miss Holland's mother had not been told, nor does Mrs Gibson know. Yet some of the schoolgirls do."

Sir Thomas put his glass down.

"You're sure?"

Masters grimaced. "I'd like to track down the leak."

Sir Thomas looked across at his son and daughter-in-law. "Did you discuss it in front of Rachel?"

"Of course not, Father."

140

"Could she have overheard you chatting about it?"

"Gr-r-umph," began Norman. "You did carry on a bit about it, Barbara."

"Carry on?" asked Kenny, quietly.

His daughter-in-law was not abashed. "I said what I thought, Father. I thought it was most unsuitable for you to marry a schoolteacher."

Sir Thomas did not lose his temper. He remained dangerously calm, but his son's wife failed to notice the pitfall.

"You thought? And why did you think that?"

"Forget it, Father," urged his son.

"Why did you think Miss Holland unsuitable?"

"A man in your position—marrying a schoolteacher. It's ridiculous."

"You needn't say any more, Barbara. You're such a bloody snob—no, purse-proud is nearer the mark—that you think a few thousand quid made out of aerated drinks and swiss rolls full of ersatz cream somehow makes you better than a woman like Mabel Holland. Why, she'd eat you, woman, socially and in every other way. You just couldn't bear the thought of any woman in my life, sharing the silly title which you covet but can never have, or inheriting what I shall have to leave because you think it is rightly yours. I knew this, when I told you the news. But you are so stupid you have to rave about it in front of Rachel. Now I don't know what part, if any, your indiscretion played in Mabel's death, but if it had any part—any at all—I shall make it my business to see you regret it."

His son stood up. "You're making too much of this, Father."

"Am I? And what did you think of my fiancée?"

"I reckoned you could do as you liked. Marry if you

141

wanted to. Marry Miss Holland if you wanted to. She was a fine woman, I thought. And damn good-looking, too."

"Did you tell your wife so?"

"Of course I did."

"And she came back at you. And Rachel overheard. All right, Norman. I know what's what. You'll excuse me if I don't see you out."

It was an awkward time of silence as Norman and Barbara left the room. When they had gone, Sir Thomas apologised to Masters and Green.

"I never liked her," he said. "She hooked Norman. God knows how. Before I knew how things were, Rachel was on the way. She'd made sure of that. And then she has the effrontery to suggest Mabel wasn't good enough to have in the family just because we've got a bob or two more than most folks. It makes you despair for the future of the human race, Mr Masters."

Masters nodded. "Even so, sir, I think you should be magnanimous. Your son obviously admired Miss Holland, so there's no need to be at loggerheads with him over this. He obviously took your side in their domestic row. And there are the children. You're fond of them, I take it?"

"Rachel and Tommy? I should just think I am."

"There you are then," said Green. "Don't make a break that would stop your seeing the kids."

"You're right." Sir Thomas finished his whisky. "Have another."

Whilst he was refilling the glasses, Masters asked him: "Do your grandchildren come round to see you, Sir Thomas? On their own, I mean. Informal visits, without their parents, at any old time?"

"Often. When I'm least expecting them. Why?"

"It occurred to me that Rachel might have called in when you were entertaining Miss Holland here."

"I don't think so."

"Could she have done without your knowing?"

"Easily." He handed them their glasses. "They just come to the side door and bowl in. Straight into the kitchen usually, to see my cook. I haven't a housekeeper. A cook and a housemaid. One elderly, the other young. They make fools of the kids."

"Then from the kitchen into the house—into any or all of the rooms—looking for you?"

"That's about the size of it." .

"I don't suppose you keep them informed of your social engagements?"

"No."

"So Rachel or Tommy *could* have called here when you were entertaining Miss Holland?"

"I suppose so."

"Or several times," said Green. "It wouldn't take long for a young girl to put two and two together and make five, being romantic at her age."

"You're making excuses for my family, and telling me I've been an old fool," said Kenny.

"No, sir. Just seeing how it might have happened that the news broke."

Kenny sat down.

"Is it relevant? That somebody knew, I mean?"

"It could be, sir."

"How?"

"I can't tell you. Should it turn out to be so, then of course you will be told."

"Thank you."

"To change the subject entirely," said Masters, "let's talk about members of the Board of Governors."

143

"What about them?"

"Each has a key to the school."

"True."

"I'll have to go round to find out if one has gone missing."

"Good heavens! Is that a possibility?"

"It's certainly a possibility we can't overlook, so we shall need a list of board members and, while we're here, we might as well start with you, Sir Thomas. Is the key still on your ring?"

"No. It never has been. I don't like carrying a load of old scrap iron around with me. I only use it about half a dozen times a year."

"I see. But you've still got it? Sorry to ask, but we have to be thorough."

Kenny got to his feet. "It's out here. It has its own ring with a white leather flap . . ." He led them into the hall to the tiny table which held the phone. He pulled open the shallow drawer. "There you are. All present and correct."

Masters glanced at Green and then turned back towards the drawing room with Sir Thomas. "I think that is all we came to see you about, sir. We'll just finish our whisky . . ."

Green followed a few feet behind, and emptied his glass with every evidence of satisfaction, to judge by the noise.

Mrs Gibson opened the door of the School House.

"Sergeant Berger, ma'am. I was here last night with Chief Inspector Green. Tonight I've brought Sergeant Reed with me. May we come in?"

"Well . . . I don't really know. There's Miss Bulmer here to go through Miss Holland's desk, to sort out all the school papers."

"We shan't disturb her."

"But what is it you want? I told you everything last night."

"Actually, Mrs Gibson, we'd just like to wait in the house. You see, we are to meet Mr Masters and Mr Green here. Mr Green told Mr Masters he ought to come and have a word with you. Well, those two had to pop over to see Sir Thomas for a few minutes and said they would drop in here to see you and pick us up on the way back."

"In that case you'd best come in."

As they were entering, a woman came out of the study and asked: "Who is it, Mrs Gibson?"

"The police, Miss Bulmer."

Reed, who was leading, introduced himself to the deputy headmistress, and nodded: "It is very convenient finding you here, Miss Bulmer."

"May I ask why?"

"I heard Superintendent Masters say only at dinner tonight that he must call on you at the first possible moment. A courtesy call, you understand, ma'am. He said it wasn't right for the police to be visiting the school without making their number with the person in charge."

"I see."

"Mr Masters will be along here shortly, to talk to Mrs Gibson. Perhaps you could see your way clear to wait until he arrives?"

"Of course I can do that. But why does he wish to see Mrs Gibson? If she is under suspicion and he intends to question her, I had better call the school solicitor."

Reed smiled. "Call him by all means, Miss. But the Chief isn't coming to interrogate Mrs Gibson. Only to meet her. I dare say he'll ask one or two little questions, but not because he suspects her of anything."

"In that case, perhaps we should sit down. In Mrs Gibson's sitting room if she will allow us. There's a fire in there."

When they were sitting down, Berger offered Miss Bulmer a cigarette.

"Do you know, I think I will. I smoke very little, but these last two or three days have been exceedingly trying."

"Cheer up," said Reed. "You've got a holiday coming."

"So I have. I'd quite forgotten that. Not that I shall get much of a holiday, I suspect. Not with things as they are."

"There'll be the funeral, too," said Mrs Gibson.

"Quite. I've asked Mrs Holland if we can wait until Monday for that so that the girls will all be away and those mistressees who are staying in Bramthorpe will be free to attend."

"Has Mrs Holland agreed?"

"Oh, yes. And the coroner."

"Good. Sergeant Berger and I visited one of your boarding houses today. Very nice they are, too. We met Miss Groombridge and . . ."

"I have had a full report, Sergeant. I understand you were tending to press quite hard questions about Miss Lickfold."

"Not really, ma'am. But we do have to consider a motive when we can. It helps."

"Naturally."

"It seems that Miss Lickfold might have had a motive. Resentment, probably."

"No," said Mrs Gibson firmly. "Not her, the poor old thing. She was always sweetness and light itself

146

with Miss Holland. I've seen and heard her, here in this house."

"There's no need to worry then, is there?" asked Reed.

"There is," said Miss Bulmer. "There is every reason to worry. I heard Mr Masters speak in court this morning. I admit I was impressed—at the time. But since then I have wondered whether he and you are not assuming there has been foul play when there has not."

"The Chief would be happier than anybody if he could prove there hasn't been, Miss Bulmer."

"But by then the damage will have been done. Probably has already been done. All the suspicion, mistrust, questioning and publicity. It will leave a scar in Bramthorpe."

"Does that mean you think there should be no investigation?"

"Not unless there is definite suspicion."

"How do you get suspicion without investigation?"

"In this case, investigation by the local police did not find any cause for suspicion. Mere whimsy brought you here."

"Wait a minute, Miss Bulmer," said Berger. "If you, as a schoolmistress, suspect—and I say suspect because you may have no definite proof—that there's something of which you don't approve going on among your girls, do you just close your eyes and hope it will go away, or do you investigate the trouble?"

"Naturally I investigate. It is my duty to do so. But if I look into the matter and find I am mistaken, I don't expect somebody else to say I am wrong and then to undertake a further and far bigger investigation."

"Even if you are not the only one to have noted the trouble? Even if one or two other people have had

147

their suspicions aroused and take a different view?"

"Give me an example of what you mean, because I cannot envisage such an eventuality."

"Right," said Berger, "I don't suppose theft is rife in Bramthorpe College . . ."

"It isn't, but we have had instances over the years."

"Suppose you begin to suspect that Mary Poppins is light-fingered. You do something about it. Perhaps you leave small sums of money about where she could easily pick them up, unseen. But she doesn't. You try it half a dozen times and the money stays safe and sound where you put it. What conclusion do you draw?"

"That I was mistaken. That Mary Poppins is honest."

"Quite. But you happen to mention to your colleagues in the staff room that you have had your suspicions about her, but have now proved beyond all doubt that Mary Poppins is honest. But one of your colleagues says, 'Wait a moment, Miss Bulmer. I haven't mentioned this to anybody because I didn't want to start a furore, but I have every reason to suspect that Mary Poppins stole my best fountain pen last week.' And then another colleague says, 'Funny you should say that, because I've kept quiet about having my watch stolen a fortnight ago, but I'm pretty sure Mary Poppins took it.' " Reed looked at Miss Bulmer. "Where money is concerned Mary Poppins is honest. But she's a magpie or jackdaw or whatever where items like pens and watches are concerned. You proved her honest. If you hadn't mentioned your test in the presence of two other mistresses who had been robbed, little Miss Mary P. would have been given an absolutely clean bill of health."

Miss Bulmer nodded. "You've made your point."

"I'd just like to add that not one of the three mistresses would have proof. In fact, just the contrary, in your case. But the suspicions of the other two—with no absolute proof—would, I feel sure, make you want to agree to a further investigation."

"You're right. I suppose I am so jealous of the school's reputation that the thought of a murder investigation which touches it—however lightly—is anathema to me."

Berger was about to reply when the front doorbell rang.

"That'll be the Chief. Shall I let him in?"

Mrs Gibson, who had been sitting quietly listening to the conversation and taking it all in without contributing much, said: "Would you? I'm getting really nervous of going to the door after dark. I don't know why. I never used to be like that."

"Shock, love," said Reed, getting to his feet. "It's natural, and it sometimes takes a while to come out."

A minute later he was back with Masters and Green.

"How are you, Mrs G?" said Green heartily. "Got quite a party here to keep you chirpy."

"I'm nicely, thank you."

"Good. Here's our boss to see you."

Masters had been introduced, by Reed, to Miss Bulmer. Now he turned to the housekeeper. "There are just one or two questions I'd like to ask you. And Miss Bulmer, too. A stroke of luck, her being here. Shall we all sit down? Berger, bring in a chair from another room, would you?"

"From the dining room," said Mrs Gibson. "That's opposite here. And don't knock the paintwork. It was only redecorated a month ago."

149

When they were finally settled, Masters said: "I understand, Mrs Gibson, that Tuesday was your day off."

"Always."

"Good. Was that fact widely known? I mean, besides yourself and Miss Holland, did anybody else know that you were away on Tuesdays—hail, rain or shine?"

"We never kept it a secret, if that's what you mean. Why should we?"

"Please don't think I'm accusing you of anything. I'm merely seeking information."

"I don't know who would know."

"I knew," said Miss Bulmer. "I cannot tell you how or why I knew or even when I learned that Mrs Gibson took Tuesdays. But I think it safe to say that every member of the staff would know. It was one of those things one learns in a community such as ours. An unimportant detail that just gets about through being mentioned in conversation."

"Miss Freeman knew, of course," said Mrs Gibson. "She came to the house so often, she'd be bound to know."

"Would such information filter through to the girls? Miss Bulmer, you could probably tell me."

"I would say the odds are that it would. Quite how, I don't know. The grapevine, I suppose."

"Because in Mrs Gibson's absence two senior girls would be called upon to make coffee for the Governors should a board meeting he held on a Tuesday?"

"That could well be one of the sources. There may be others. You see, everybody was aware of Mrs Gibson's presence. Not that any of us saw her all that often, but she was known to be here, in the background, looking after Miss Holland. And believe me, Mr Masters, if you had ever met our late headmistress, you would know that she was well cared for. She had that air about her. A lovely-looking woman, in her prime, with everything about her just right. Not prim. She looked well fed—not because she was plump, but because she looked a picture of health. She was well turned out. Not because she spent a fortune on clothes, but because those she had were well chosen and well cared for. Of course she had the happy knack of being able to work through a hard day and to emerge at the end of it looking as she had done at nine o'clock in the morning. The rest of us finish a day with our hair awry, chalk on our fingers and in our nails, probably with a tear in our gowns where we've caught them on some protuberance, exhausted with putting over our lessons and sore-footed through standing to teach through long periods. Miss Holland was different. One just knew, by looking at her, that she had the back-up forces to care for her. That she hadn't had to go home to housework the night before, and she wouldn't have to go home to housework tonight either. That is how Mrs Gibson looked after her and put her out on parade each day. It was a point nobody could have missed."

"There's a glowing tribute for you, Mrs G.," said Green. "Unsolicited testimonial."

"We did our best, and we were very happy doing it."

"I'm sure you were," said Masters. "Now, another question. Presumably you went out at times other than for the whole day on Tuesdays?"

"To shop you mean?"

"I was thinking more of your social activities. In the evenings. Did you ever go to the cinema or a church guild or anything like that after dinner at night?"

"Oh, quite often. Not to the pictures or church, but I went out to visit my friends or they came here. Mostly I went out. When Miss Holland didn't need me I was free to go any night."

"Would anybody other than Miss Holland know when you were going out to visit your friends?"

"I don't see how they could."

Masters looked round sharply as Miss Bulmer opened her mouth and made a sound as though she were about to speak and had then decided against it.

"Yes, Miss Bulmer?"

"I have no wish to contradict Mrs Gibson, but I was aware of the fact that most Thursday evenings she went over to Groombridge. She and the matron were friends. . . ."

"That's right," agreed Mrs Gibson. "But it wasn't regular. Not absolutely. I used to pop over to see Matron—she lives in Groombridge, you see, though she's matron for all three houses—but I didn't go if Miss Holland was entertaining for instance."

"I see," said Masters. "But would the visits be regular enough for somebody who knew, say, that Miss Holland was going out to dinner, to be sure you would be out of the house, too?"

"I suppose they would, really."

"Thank you."

"But it depends who you mean by somebody?"

"I suppose I mean everybody. All the girls in Groombridge, for example. They must have noticed you coming and going between their house and here."

"And in the other two houses," said Reed. "All the back windows look this way across the playing field. There can't be many people use that path at any time, let alone in the evening when the whole place is

152

locked up. So Mrs Gibson's comings and goings could easily be noted."

Mrs Gibson asked: "What has all this got to do with Miss Holland being dead? Little things that I did, like going to see Matron? Are you telling me I helped to kill her?"

"Emphatically not," said Masters sternly, to the surprise of Reed and Berger. "I shall get cross if you start thinking anything of the kind. I am asking questions. I am not accusing or suspecting you. You heard what Miss Bulmer said about the way you cared for Miss Holland. Everybody must know that you would never do anything to displease her, let alone harm her. I expect, even, that she was glad you went over to visit the matron."

"She was."

"There you are then."

"She said it was good for two old fogeys like her and me to get out of the house as often as we could." Mrs Gibson could scarcely finish what she said because of the tears that started to flow. "Two old fogeys like us . . . But she didn't live to be old . . ."

"Come on, love," said Green, moving over to put an arm round the housekeeper's shoulder. "You heard what Mr Masters said. You don't want him to get cross with you. Or me. So come on. Sergeant Berger will get you a glass of sherry." He nodded to the sergeant, who went off to do his bidding. "Here you are now. Use my hanky. That little thing of yours is no earthly. It looks as if it had been out in a thunderstorm already. Come on. Stop crying and dry the tears."

As Green comforted the housekeeper, Masters asked Miss Bulmer: "Once the boarders finish school or

153

games and get back to their houses, are they confined for the rest of the evening until bedtime?"

"There is no short answer to that question."

"Supply me with a long one, then."

"In theory, all the girls in the boarding houses are supposed to remain within the school bounds at all times except for excursions for which mistresses are responsible, or outings for which special leave is asked and granted. That gives the school authorities the whip hand, and is necessary because we are *in loco parentis* at all times of the day and night.

"As I said, that is in theory. In practice, Miss Holland relaxed her own regulations. Rightly, in my view, she pointed out that in a school which has both day girls and boarders, the day girls get privileges which, if we adhered strictly to our rules, boarders would not enjoy. The parents of day girls take them out and about and, particularly in the case of the senior girls, allow them a great freedom of unsupervised movement. They have boyfriends and go to discos and so on. To be deprived of this freedom in this day and age, would be a source of discontent among our boarders. So, Miss Holland introduced what she called her 'blind-eye' supervision clause.

"Put at its simplest, this clause means that all boarders who are not engaged in school team matches are free after lunch on Saturdays throughout the year. But reporting-back times are earlier in the winter, particularly for the younger girls. They have to be back by half-past five in winter, half-past eight in summer. Older girls are allowed out until nine in winter, ten in summer. Those who come home late are not allowed out the next week."

"Saturdays are the only days they are allowed out?"

"No. After lunch on Sundays, too. But in winter

everybody must be back in time for evening chapel. In summer—because so many parents visit on a Sunday —these rules are relaxed at the discretion of the house-mistress.

"At other times—that is on ordinary weekdays— senior girls have Tuesday afternoons free, juniors have Thursday afternoons free. In the winter terms, nobody gets out in the evenings except in chaperoned parties. In the summer terms, tennis and athletics and swimming are allowed after prep."

"In the school grounds?"

"Oh yes. We have all the facilities here. I have only given you a brief outline of our free time activities, but you must realise that all the school's clubs and societies meet, at their various times, within the school bounds. Life-saving classes for instance are on Wednes-day evenings for the seniors. The juniors do their saving between the end of chapel and lunch on Sun-days. Play rehearsals are put in at all sorts of odd times, including Saturday evenings. The same with music.

"So, though the place may sound like a prison, Miss Holland had established a system which gave our boarders a great deal of freedom." She smiled at Masters. "So many things have to be thought of in a girls' school. Take Matron as a case in point. Can you imagine the trouble she has in supervising the shampooing of a hundred and fifty heads of hair every week? To say nothing of ensuring that some little Misses are not dodging the column over the daily tub?"

Masters shrugged. "Complicated," he said.

"It sounds it when one tries to describe it. But Miss Holland's blind-eye clause really helped with disci-pline among the boarders. Because of it, there were privileges the girls could lose if they did not toe the line. Very few of them were naughty."

"So discipline was strict and punishments were few?"

"That is a slightly different question, but in the main you are right. Miss Holland had very precise views on punishments."

"I heard she had introduced a punishment book."

"Ah, yes! That was for a specific, domestic reason, but it played a part in her philosophy. She insisted that we distinguish very clearly between punishments for misbehaviour and those for bad work. For the former she instituted the punishment book you mentioned. For the latter, the detention book."

"I hadn't heard of that."

"Detention was the more serious matter. Misbehaviour had really to merit punishment and that, when set, had to take the form of extra written work closely connected with the curriculum. But Miss Holland was not keen on this."

"Why?"

"She took the view that every young person was mischievous to a greater or lesser degree. Any teacher worth her salt should be able to recognise this and to deal with it by force of character rather than by resorting to impositions. She recognised there would be times when even the best teacher might fail—hence the punishment book. But when it came to bad work, then she became really concerned. She obliged mistresses to discover why the work was bad. Was it because something had been badly taught and the pupil didn't understand it? Was the girl herself not up to the work being taught and set? Had the girl merely skimped her prep? If so, why? Was she worried, or ill, or diverted in some way?"

156

"In other words, a reason had to be found."

"Quite. Then, if the bad work was really the girl's own fault—with no extenuating circumstances—it was brought home to her that the school would not accept it, that mistresses were not going to waste time in teaching, setting and marking work which the girl was too idle to do."

"Detention?"

"A lot of extra work, in school, on her half day. Supervised by the duty mistress. But worse than that—and here the seriousness came into it—a score of three detentions in any one term could lead to parents being requested to remove the girl in question. Certainly, if the bad work continued into a second term, the girl would be required to go. So you see, the detention book was an important document, with each entry supported by written reasons for the detention and notes on the investigation into the causes of the bad work. The result was that we had a very sound discipline under Miss Holland, but the punishments available to us were comparatively rarely used."

"It sounds most enlightened. A benevolent dictatorship, in fact. Were any girls ever expelled?"

"Yes. In Miss Holland's first year there was a certain amount of weeding out. But there has been no need for it recently. You see, Mr Masters, no girl was punished if she genuinely could not do her work. If that happened, we kept her back a year to allow her to catch up. It almost invariably worked and the girl in question was always happier at being given the chance to cope."

Masters said: "I would like to see the detention book."

"For any particular reason?"

"Nosiness. I've seen the punishment book."

"Miss Holland kept the detention book locked away in her study."

"Here, in the house study?"

"Yes. It was too important to leave in school."

"Excellent. I shall be able to see it before I go. Thank you, Miss Bulmer. You've been a mine of information."

"You mean I've helped you?"

"Most assuredly." Before the deputy headmistress could press him further, he turned to Green who was sitting close to Mrs Gibson. They were smoking and chatting, and the storm of grief seemed to be safely over. "How are we doing now?" he asked.

"We're all right, it's them others," said Green laconically.

"Good. Now, Mrs Gibson, please don't get upset, but we're going to inspect your kitchen."

"You what? You're not suggesting there's anything wrong with my kitchen! If you are, you've got another think coming."

"Perhaps. But nevertheless I'd like my sergeant to inspect your cupboards."

"What for?"

"We shall know that if we find anything."

"You won't find anything that isn't sweet and good."

"I'm not saying we shall. But just in case we do, would you like to be present? And you, Miss Bulmer? To befriend Mrs Gibson and—almost—as an independent witness?"

Miss Bulmer got to her feet. "I feel it would be right for me to be present."

"Excellent. Shall we go? Lead on, please, Mrs Gibson, but please touch nothing. Just answer questions."

"This sounds exceedingly serious," said Miss Bulmer.

"Come on, love," Green urged her. "Use your nous. We've got to examine the house carefully. Where better to start than the kitchen, since it was something she ate that killed Miss Holland?"

Miss Bulmer drew herself up as though to indicate that—even if only temporarily—the school premises, including this house, were her property, and she would like this to be recognised and policemen not to address her as "love". Her attitude didn't get through to Green, who continued: "Trust the Super not to cause unnecessary trouble or distress. If he says search the kitchen, he has a good reason for doing so."

"What does he hope to find?"

"Hope? Or expect?"

"The latter."

"You'd be surprised. At least I expect I shall."

Mrs Gibson led them to the kitchen door and pressed the switch. A tube on the ceiling flickered, waned momentarily and then sprang to full life to show a room which, though basically old, had been modernised quite recently with all the units and gadgets that—according to standpoint—make life easier or more complicated and expensive.

"Nice," said Green. "Who chose the colours, Mrs G? White, almond green and chestnut. Tasteful."

"What is it you want to see?" asked Mrs Gibson, obviously in no mood to respond further to Green's joshing.

"The cupboard in which you keep all your supplies of spices, gravy browning and such like, please."

Mrs Gibson snorted. "You'll find nothing there that shouldn't be there."

"Which cupboard please?"

"The last one under the working-top on the left. The one this side of the tall one."

"Lift each item out carefully," ordered Masters. "Use handkerchiefs. You take them out, Berger. One at a time. You open them, Reed. Get a knife or spoon handle to ease the lids off. Inspect the contents carefully."

There was just one shelf of the cupboard rammed with all shapes and sizes of drums, small bottles, sprinkle tops, packets, tubes and sachets.

"Oxo cubes," said Berger, lifting three packets of the familiar meatblocks out of the cupboard and putting them on the top. Parmesan, dried sage and garlic granules followed in quick succession.

"Steady," grumbled Reed. He was prising lids off, sniffing, dipping his little finger in and tasting before pushing each item away.

"I don't know what you expect to find," said Mrs Gibson: "All I know is you won't find it."

"Hold it," growled Reed. He was holding a largish drum. "This says cornflour, Chief. But if this ever went into gravy it would set it like cement. I think it's one of the patent plasters by the taste of it."

Masters moved forward and took the cardboard drum in his own handkerchief. He examined the contents and then showed them to Green.

"Thistlefix," said the D.C.I. emphatically, naming one of the packet plaster-powders. "I use it about my house for bunging up holes."

"Please don't try to touch the drum," said Masters, holding out the container to Mrs Gibson, "but examine the contents. Taste them if you like."

Mrs Gibson wrinkled her nose in disgust. "That's never my cornflour."

"Nevertheless it is in a cornflour drum in your spice cupboard."

"I never put it there."

"I'm sure you didn't." Masters put the drum on one side. "Anything else, Reed?"

"This, sir. It says 'chilli powder', but it looks more like brick dust."

"It's a powder colour," said Miss Bulmer. "For water painting."

"It's what?" gasped Mrs Gibson. "How'd that get there? Miss Holland liked her chilli con carne . . ."

"And this, sir. Should be red pepper, but it isn't." He showed Masters a small drum of what should have been paprika.

"What's going on?" wailed Mrs Gibson.

"White pepper O.K.," said Reed. Then—

"Hello, Chief. These look wrong to me."

"What?"

"It says black peppercorns, but I don't reckon they are."

"Careful," warned Masters. "I think they may be what we want."

"Laburnum seeds for a bet," grunted Green, peering into the cardboard cylinder. "I don't know what laburnum seeds look like, but I know what peppercorns look like. We have one of those little mills at home and I'm always having to fill it."

"Finish off," said Masters to Reed. "And then box up the suspects. I want every one of them tested for prints. And I want it done by you and Berger. Don't let the locals get their hands on them."

"We could do it here, Chief. The bags are in the boot of the car."

Reed was referring to the murder bags which the Yard teams invariably carried with them on investigations. They contained all manner of implements, including the insufflators and brushes for dusting surfaces for prints and the cameras for taking dab graphs.

"Very well. But as it is now getting late, don't be too long about it. The rest of us will go back to Mrs Gibson's room."

Once Masters, Green and the two women were back in the little sitting room, Masters lost no time in getting down to business.

"Now, Mrs Gibson, what you have just seen came as a great surprise to you?"

"Of course it did. You don't think I'd have things like paint powders among my flavourings, do you?"

"But they were there, nevertheless."

"I didn't put them there."

"Let me reassure you. I know you didn't put them there. But I need your help in deciding who did."

"I can't tell you, can I?"

"Leave it to me. How often do you use those items?"

"Not often. They're there for use when we want them. Some have been there for years. The others . . . Well, we use the gravy powder a lot, and the Bovril and Oxo. But stuff like chilli powder, that's more in winter."

"What about the black peppers?"

"We have a mill—like Mr Green said he had. We fill it up when it gets empty."

"How often is that?"

"Once a month? I don't know. I don't keep count."

"Infrequently, at any rate?"

"Yes."

"When did you last fill it?"

"Can't remember. Not in the last week or ten days."

"Excellent." Masters turned to Green. "Find it, please, Bill. Examine the contents."

"It's next to the cruet and salad cream in the side-board in the dining room."

Green nodded his thanks and left.

162

Masters turned to Miss Bulmer. "Does anything about this strike you as strange for a major crime, but familiar to you as a schoolmistress?"

Miss Bulmer, grave-faced, replied reluctantly. "It has all the earmarks of a prank. I have known similar things happen in the boarding houses where mischievous girls mixed salt with the sugar. Harmless enough in those cases. But pranks, none the less."

Masters nodded his agreement. Mrs Gibson said: "Girls! None of the girls would do it. They all liked her. Besides, how could they? How could they get in to the kitchen to do it?"

Masters ignored this outburst. He said, instead: "I shall need examples of Miss Holland's fingerprints. Some private book with the right surface or paper she was working on . . ."

Green came back.

"Genuine peppers," he said. "Half full."

"Thank you."

"There you are then," said Mrs Gibson. "She couldn't have got it from there. I don't know how she could have eaten them. I don't really. It's beyond me."

Masters paused for a moment, and then said: "Was Miss Holland a good cook?"

"Only so-so. She didn't have to be. I did it all."

"Quite. But you did good family cooking, didn't you? Roasts, pies, casseroles. That sort of thing?"

"Yes."

"English cooking?"

"Yes."

"Yet Miss Holland, according to you, liked chilli con carne. Now that is not originally an English dish. So how did you come to make that for her?"

"I'd never heard of it. But she said it was a good alternative to curry if we'd got some left-over meat to mince up. She always ate it with just a fork, but I like putting on a meal you have to use a knife with."

"Miss Holland herself never suggested foreign dishes?"

"Like what?"

"Boeuf stroganoff, bouillabaisse . . ."

"Not to me she didn't."

"Did she ever try her hand at them?"

"I told you, she didn't have to cook except on Tuesdays if she wasn't going out."

"Please don't get upset. My questions have a purpose. Did you ever know her, on a Tuesday, to cook something that you wouldn't normally cook for her?"

"Never."

"Are there any cookery books in the house?"

"We have a bag with a lot of stuff in. Two books and a lot of recipes cut out of papers and that sort of thing. But we never use any of them."

"Bag?"

"One of these plastic ones with a zip. Document bags, I think they're called. Miss Holland always got them given to her when she went to conferences and meetings—with papers in."

"I know the sort of thing. Where is it kept?"

"On one of the little shelves in the alcove in the kitchen."

"Do you want me to get it?" asked Green.

"It's navy blue. Just behind the fan."

Green looked at her. "We have a fan we can plug in when it gets hot in the kitchen. We keep it on that shelf."

"I see."

When Green came back, he was accompanied by Reed. "We shall need Mrs Gibson's prints, Chief, and Miss Holland's."

"Mine? Why mine?"

"So that we can see whose prints should be on those drums and whose shouldn't, love. You and Miss Holland were entitled to handle them. We want to be sure we get them sorted out."

"That's right, Mrs Gibson. We shan't keep them on file once we've used them. They'll be burned as soon as we've finished the case."

"I don't like it."

"Quite right," said Green. "It's a shame when a woman like you has to be mixed up in this sort of thing through no fault of your own. And we don't like involving you, either. But somebody mucked about with the things in your kitchen, didn't they? And we've got to find out who it was. You're going to help us, I know. Come on, now. It's a messy business. You'll get ink on your fingers, but it'll wash off. Go with Sergeant Reed to the kitchen, there's a love. Two minutes and it'll all be over."

Mrs Gibson got to her feet.

"Go into Miss Holland's study," Masters said to Reed. "You should be able to get Miss Holland's prints from something in there. Failing that, you'll have to visit the morgue and take prints from the body."

"Right, Chief. Come along, Mrs Gibson."

As soon as the housekeeper had left the room, Green handed the blue plastic document case over to Masters. "I've held it by the corner only."

"Thanks. If I hold it by the other corner, could you unzip it?"

Green did as he was asked and Masters gingerly edged the contents out. "The sergeants had better go over the bag."

Again Green departed. Masters went straight for the

bigger and glossier of the two cookery books. He opened the back cover to consult the index.

"What are you looking for?" asked Miss Bulmer. "Surely you can't find evidence in there."

"No? Well, perhaps not." Masters found what he was looking for. "Page 128." He righted the book and opened it. Between pages 128 and 129 was an empty, used envelope.

"A bookmark?"

"It would seem so, Miss Bulmer." Masters picked it up and handed it to the deputy headmistress.

"Can you read the postmark?"

Miss Bulmer peered at it. "Posted in Bramthorpe at twelve-thirty on October the . . . Good heavens, Superintendent! This was posted last Monday, the day before Miss Holland died." She looked up at him. "How on earth did you know . . .?"

"I didn't know. It's just a stroke of luck. But I think I shall be right to assume that the letter which that envelope contained arrived at the house on Tuesday morning and that on Tuesday evening Miss Holland used it as a bookmark. Mrs Gibson was away all day on Tuesday so I must assume that she would not consult the cookery book and, therefore, did not use the envelope to mark the page."

"I see that. But why should Miss Holland use it?"

Green rejoined them. "Use what?" he asked.

Masters told him of the envelope. Green whistled gently to express amazement, satisfaction and every other emotion involved in the reception of such a find.

"Why should Miss Holland use it?" demanded Miss Bulmer a second time.

"Do you know a great deal about Miss Holland's social life?" countered Masters.

cides on one. She picks up an envelope from the
esk or from the waste-paper basket to mark the place.
hen she puts the other books and cuttings back in
e bag and she carries them all to the kitchen to be-
in her chores She lays the bag on the kitchen table
nd opens the book at the chosen recipe. She cooks
er steak, thinks how good it looks. Closes the recipe
ook with a flourish, leaving the envelope still in it,
nd returns the whole lot to the shelf in the alcove
where Mrs Gibson keeps them. Then she eats her
steak, and some time later begins to feel unwell."

Miss Bulmer smiled at him. "It is a very graphic
account, but you haven't got second sight. You can't
be sure that is what happened."

"He can, love," said Green quietly.

"Nonsense."

"Have a look at the recipe it was marking." Green
held the book out to her.

For a moment or two she stared. Then—

"Steak au Poivre! Peppered Steak," she murmured.

"Look at the ingredients and the instructions," said
Green. "One tablespoonful of crushed peppercorns.
To be pressed into both sides of the steak which is
hen fried and served with cream and brandy. But for
eppercorns in this case, substitute laburnum seeds.
ot unlike peppercorns and, coming from a pepper-
rn drum, easily mistaken for them, especially if, not
specting anything, you don't look very closely, or
u drop them straight out of the drum into the
pper part of the electric mixer. Who is to tell what
y are when they come out crushed?"

After Green finished speaking, there was a long
nce.

It's unbelievable," said Miss Bulmer.

"Only what she saw fit to tell me. When she was
going to official or semi-official functions for instance,
or where she intended to spend her holidays."

"She said very little about her personal relationships
with friends?"

"I wasn't aware that she had many close friends—
not round here, at any rate. A woman in her position
was bound to make numerous acquaintances, to receive
many invitations and to entertain a good deal in return. But I never heard that she was particularly close
to anybody."

"Thank you. Now to change the subject. Tell me
what you thought when you heard today that Miss
Holland had some momentous news for her mother.
What did you imagine that news could be?"

"What do you think it was?"

"I am asking for ideas from you," said Masters
gently. "I believe that the knowledge of what that
news was could be central to this case, so naturally I
want the ideas of people on the spot."

"The only guess I can hazard is that she had been
offered some very senior post in the academic world.
By that I mean, the headship of one of the women's
colleges at either Oxford or Cambridge or, alternative-
ly, that she was to become the first woman Vice Chan-
cellor of one of the other universities. I cannot believe
that anything else would take her from Bramthorpe."

"And you think she would be overjoyed by this?
That she would suggest that it would delight her
mother?"

"I must confess that part of your disclosure surprised me a little when I heard it. Professional women
of Miss Holland's calibre would normally take any
furtherance of their careers more calmly—with more

quiet satisfaction shall we say—than the letter to her mother suggested."

"In that case," said Masters, "could it be something in her private—as opposed to professional—life that occasioned the personal delight she expressed?"

"I can't imagine what it could be."

"Think, Miss Bulmer. Forget Miss Holland was a headmistress. What news would a daughter normally hurry home to impart to her mother? News of such a nature that her mother would be delighted by it?"

Miss Bulmer opened her eyes in surprise. "Well, now, I can think of only two things—marriage or approaching motherhood."

"I hardly imagine Miss Holland would be happy to announce the latter," said Masters drily.

"In that case . . ." Miss Bulmer stared even harder. "In that case, you must think she was about to marry. Are you seriously suggesting that as the answer?"

"Can you think of any other solution that would fill the bill?"

"Who to? Or should I say to whom?"

"Ah!" said Masters. "Now that is another question. I've only been in Bramthorpe for little more than twenty-four hours. How could I possibly know that if you, her close colleague for all of her time here, have no inkling of the identity of the man?"

"Well, I haven't. So I don't think I believe your solution."

"No?"

"An item of local news like that could never have been kept quiet unless . . ."

"Yes?"

"Unless it was a man who does not live here. Somebody who lives elsewhere and whom Miss Holland

knew before she came to Bramthorpe. Perh[aps] [an] old friend who has now secured a divorce o[r be]come a widower. . . ."

"All are possibilities," acknowledged Maste[rs]. Miss Bulmer shook her head. "No. I still d[on't be]lieve it. Miss Holland would not give up Bra[mthorpe] for marriage."

"Would she have had to? Is there anything [to pre]vent a married woman being a headmistress? A[fter all] we have a married woman as Prime Minister. . [. ."

"I think the Governors of Bramthorpe woul[dn't] take kindly to a married woman."

"You would know. But the answer is immat[erial.] You asked me why I thought Miss Holland should [use] this envelope as a bookmark in the cookery book[. I'll] tell you. Whatever the reason for it, Miss Holland [was] a happy woman. Particularly happy at just that [mo]ment on Tuesday when, all alone, she starts to t[hink] about the dinner she has to cook for herself. She [has] not been invited out, but feels a bit too happy ju[st to] cook and eat the steak Mrs Gibson has brought i[n. Or] should she take herself out to dinner? No, becaus[e she] finds the prospect of eating out alone unattra[ctive,] particularly in her happy mood. So what shou[ld she] do? Then the idea strikes her. She will eat the [steak] but she will prepare it in some more esoteric wa[y than] just grilling it. The question is, how? The an[swer is] to get out the cookery books and choose a [recipe.] Though not a greatly accomplished cook, sh[e is no]body's fool, and she will be able to follow [a recipe] easily enough. So she goes to the kitchen—[or the] study where she has been sitting—and fetch[es a pile] of books. She pores over the pages, consid[ering] one and that one among the recipes until [. . ."

"It's what happened, love. Can you think of any other way of getting a handful of crushed laburnum seeds down the throat of somebody like your Miss Holland?"

"I must confess I can't."

"See how the sergeants are getting on, Bill. It's nearly midnight."

"I would rather you kept your counsel about everything you have heard here tonight, Miss Bulmer. Have I your word?"

"I shall regard your request as an instruction."

"Thank you. In return I promise to deal as lightly as I can with the school. In any case, I shall keep you fully informed, and tomorrow I shall come to see you again. It's a full day in school, I believe?"

"Yes."

"Excellent. When I call, we can meet in the headmistress's study. You will be using that now, won't you?"

"That is my intention."

"Now, please, if I could have the detention book . . .?"

Green came back. "They've finished. They're helping Mrs G. to put back the bits and pieces in her study. They've got what they wanted from a cheque book. I don't suppose anybody else ever handled that."

"Good. We'd better be getting along. We've still got some talking to do."

"As long as there's some beer left . . ."

"The prints," said Reed, once the beer had been poured and they were settled in Masters' room, "show that three people with smaller fingers handled those drums. Mrs Gibson's fingers are quite fat. Miss Holland's were slim, but of a capable size. The others are smaller and, to my thinking, could be those of kids."

"I don't like it," said Green glumly. "Not kids. Little lasses playing pranks. And doing away with a woman like Miss Holland. It's all wrong."

"Yes, Chief," said Reed. "What are you hoping to do? Line them all up and take their dabs? That's going to cause some trouble if you do. You'd have to get their parents' permission."

"Questions in the House even if you tried," added Berger. "Involving children—innocent children, as they all are, except three—in police murder procedures! Disgusting. The powers of the police must be curbed."

Masters drew on his pipe. "I agree with the D.C.I. I am not a little dismayed by the thought that a comparatively harmless prank on the part of three probably angelic fourteen-year-old kids, results in death for anyone, be they of the calibre of Miss Holland or less. But what do I do? Bow out? Pretend it didn't happen?"

"You're in a dilemma, right enough," said Green. "You've got to go ahead. No option. But I'd like . . ."

"Yes?"

"Look, George. I'm a stupid old fool. I'm as keen on nailing villains as anybody. I ought to be, because I've spent all my adult life doing it. But when it comes to kids and murder investigations I don't like myself all that much."

"You were saying you would like something or other."

"Yeah! I'd like to put this business to Hildidge. To Sir Thomas, even. Consult them about it, because though I'm sure you're right and some of the school girls are involved, we haven't yet proved it. And to ask permission to fingerprint hundreds of kids without a proven case . . ."

"How can I prove my case if I'm not allowed to investigate it by all the normal means at my disposal? Besides, it is unlikely that we would need to print all the girls. We would discover the ones involved before we came to the end."

"That's true. But even the request to parents is going to cause an almighty stink round here, and as we are all opposed to it . . ."

Masters got to his feet.

"Thanks," he said quietly. "You've helped me—all of you."

"We have, Chief?"

Masters grinned. "I was temperamentally opposed to seeking permission to fingerprint three hundred school pupils. But I thought that if I said so you'd all jump down my throat for being so concerned about it. But you've all come out on my side. Furthermore the D.C.I. has made an excellent suggestion—one which hadn't occurred to me—that we should put the whole business, as it now stands, into the hands of the locals. Tomorrow, you will be able to hand over to them the photographs of the prints. We could then tell our story and bow out, leaving all the rest to them . . ."

"To Lovegrove?" snorted Green. "He'd make a pig's ear of it. He'd chase those kids rotten to get his case tied up."

"The D.C.I.'s right, Chief."

"Very well. What you are all saying is that I should report to Hildidge. Tell him how things stand. And then offer him the alternative to either asking parents' consent to printing the whole school or leaving us free to arrive at the answer in some other way."

"If we can do that," said Green, "we could always use the prints we've got to confirm we've picked out the right ones. Then there's no objection. Pick your little villains and take their dabs to confirm their guilt or prove their innocence."

Masters nodded. "The whole lot of us has gone soft."

"Maybe we have," growled Green. "But if you and Wanda had a little daughter at this school—completely innocent in every way—would you give consent for blokes like us to ink her fingers, with a murder rap looming in the near distance?"

Masters looked across at Green.

"As a matter of fact . . ."

"Yes?"

"I'm delighted to hear you say all this. I thought I might have been affected in my view by the thought of approaching fatherhood. I now find . . ."

"You what?" demanded Green explosively. "You? And Wanda? You mean Wanda's expecting a baby?"

"Yes."

"Why the devil didn't you tell us? My missus will be over the moon when I tell her. You know what she thinks of Wanda."

"We only knew for certain the day before yesterday. I was leaving it for Wanda to tell you herself."

Green grinned. "The little beauty," he breathed. "Doris and I . . . Well, I don't have to tell you that we're both crackers about your missus. We only really tolerate you because of her. Here! I'd better ring Doris and tell her."

"At after one o'clock in the morning?" asked Reed.

"I expect Wanda will have told her by now," said Masters.

174

"Oh yes, of course," said Green. He addressed Berger. "Here, lad, is there any more beer?"

"None left."

"Dammit, I wanted to drink a toast."

CHAPTER VI

Friday was a wet day. People were wearing raincoats and scurrying about under umbrellas as Reed drove the Yard team to the local police station. Two phone calls made immediately after breakfast had been enough to ensure that Hildidge and Sir Thomas Kenny would both be in the former's office by half-past nine. All six men assembled almost to the minute. The Chief Superintendent had seen to it that there were enough chairs and ashtrays for his guests.

When they were all seated, Hildidge said to Masters: "You told me that you had satisfied yourself that Miss Holland's death was neither suicide nor accidental death in what we, as policemen, would regard as the normal use of the words. Please explain that."

"I would rather it came out in the course of our conversation so that it will be self-explanatory, and also to avoid giving you our report back to front."

"You've asked Sir Thomas to be present, too. May I know the significance of that?"

Masters paused a moment before replying. Then—

"Perhaps I should tell you that it would be possible to identify the villains in this particular piece inside an hour—given the opportunity. That we have not done this is due to a delicacy of feeling on our part; to some degree of consideration for the feelings of both you gentlemen; and the fact that we haven't, as yet, sought the opportunity."

"Consideration for our feelings? As citizens of standing in Bramthorpe, you mean? Sir Thomas because he is Chairman of the School Governors and the Watch Committee and I because I am responsible for law and order in the town?"

"Partly that, sir. But I was referring particularly to your feelings as father and grandfather respectively."

Sir Thomas sat bolt upright. "What's that? My feelings as a grandfather? That sounds to me as though you are saying little Rachel is involved. And that is something I will not believe."

"And my daughter Helen," said Hildidge angrily. "My lass isn't involved either. Not with Miss Holland's death, and nobody will tell me different."

"There you are, George," said Green airily. "I told you what it would be like. And these two gentlemen are on our side. What three hundred parents who weren't on our side would be like is beyond belief. Shows how wise we were to come here before making any move."

"What the hell are you talking about?" asked Hildidge. "Three hundred? What three hundred?"

"Perhaps," said Masters, "I had better tell you something of our investigations."

Hildidge grunted and Sir Thomas said: "Perhaps you had."

"Last evening, in the School House, in the presence of Mrs Gibson and Miss Bulmer, we examined a cupboard in the kitchen. The shelf we chose to examine—for obvious reasons—was the one holding all the drums of flavourings and spices that one finds in a well-run kitchen. You will both be familiar with what I mean —drums of herbs, dried mint, sage; little shakers of paprika, chilli powder, garlic granules; boxes of gravy browning, Oxo cubes, Bovril, Marmite. I needn't go on.

"Among those drums was one of cornflour—but a patent form of plaster powder had been substituted for its original contents. Chilli powder and paprika had been emptied away, and in their place had been put similarly coloured water-colour paint powders. There were, I think, five substitutions. The most important of all was the black peppercorn drum. Laburnum seeds had been substituted for the corns."

"Good God Almighty!" said Kenny.

"Quite, sir." Misters waited a moment before continuing. Then he said: "It was all very well to discover the source of the laburnum seeds, but it was quite another problem to decide exactly how Miss Holland had come to ingest so many."

"In mistake for pepper, of course," said Hildidge.

"Just so, sir. But there were so many found in her system that it ruled out—to my mind—an ordinary use of pepper. However, once I remembered that Mrs Gibson had provided steak for Miss Holland's supper, I was able to link steak and peppercorns together and come up with Steak au Poivre which, as you will doubtless remember, requires a tablespoonful or so of crushed peppercorns in the cooking."

"That's just guesswork," said Hildidge.

"It was—at first. But when we examined a recipe book at the School House, we found the page for Peppered Steak had been marked with a used envelope. The letter had been posted last Monday, as the date stamp clearly shows. It could only have reached Miss Holland on Tuesday—the day of her death. Mrs Gibson was not present to use the book on Tuesday, nor has she used it since. Miss Holland was the only one who could have used the envelope and that, without a doubt, means that she prepared herself Steak au Poivre with laburnum seeds instead of peppers."

"So it was an accident after all," said Hildidge.

"No, sir. Miss Holland may not have recognised the seeds for what they were, but they closely resemble peppers, and that drum was supposed to contain peppers. She had as much right to believe they were genuine as a man at a bar has a right to believe that the drink he has bought is good and wholesome and not laced with knock-out drops."

"Quite right," said Kenny.

"You're a policeman, Mr Hildidge," said Masters, "so you know what's coming next. We had handled those drums with great care, so we were able to fingerprint them. Reed and Berger are both trained in the art and the waxed board from which such receptacles are made provides an ideal surface for taking and holding prints. We also took Mrs Gibson's prints and recovered a full set of Miss Holland's from one of her personal cheque books.

"The result is that we have now sorted out three sets of strange prints and, although he cannot be absolutely sure of this, Reed thinks that they are what he describes as coming from immature people."

"Girls, I suppose?" said Hildidge.

"But not necessarily girls from the school," insisted Kenny.

Masters bowed his head to acknowledge the truth of Sir Thomas' comment. Green, however, was not prepared to let such a facile truth pass unremarked.

"Mixing those substances up and substituting some for others was a prank," he said. "A schoolkid's prank. And when you're looking for the perpetrators of a schoolkid's prank you don't ignore the presence of three hundred schoolgirls right there on the spot. If you did, you'd be daft and you'd be in a hell of a hole. If you were to ignore the obvious, where would you start looking for three other kids? At some school a mile away?"

Kenny seemed a little startled at Green's tone but he was gracious enough to say that he saw the force of the D.C.I.'s remarks and had not intended to suggest that Bramthorpe girls could be excluded from suspicion.

"I know you didn't," replied Green. "You're worried about this. You've a grandchild whom you dote on at the school. As chairman you're responsible for its good name. And to crown it all you've lost a particularly close friend in Miss Holland. Mr Hildidge is worried, too, for much the same reasons. And so are we worried. That's why we are here."

Masters turned to Hildidge. "At last you know why I said that Miss Holland's death was neither suicide nor accident in the accepted sense of the word. Now we must try to convey to you why we asked to see you, with Sir Thomas present. As I said, I could most probably identify the owners of those immature prints within an hour—but that would mean taking the fingerprints of every girl in the school."

"Take my Helen's prints? And Sir Thomas' Rachel's?"

"Together with those of two hundred and ninety-eight others, all of whom, except possibly three, are completely uninvolved in this business," replied Masters.

"I don't like it. In fact, Superintendent, the law forbids it."

"Not specifically, sir. It allows us to seek parental consent. But apart from any hint of indiscriminate

181

fingerprinting, we—that is all the members of my team besides myself—are totally opposed to the idea of seeking consent. But this is your patch, sir, and it is your case. That is why we have come to you. We can prove there is a case and we believe we can solve it quickly. But only by the means we've just discussed. If we do not check the fingerprints, then we must go a different way and try to identify our culprits by other means. The choice is yours."

Hildidge looked across at Sir Thomas. "We have to be very careful about whom we fingerprint. There are strict rules about it, and we would think more than twice before we asked permission to take prints from a child. We would certainly never contemplate taking those from the whole school."

"But in a case like murder . . .?"

"The most serious crime in the calendar, Sir Thomas. One in which the police pull out all the stops. Mr Masters would never be censured officially were he to circularise the parents asking for their permission to go ahead."

"Unofficially?"

"There would be an outcry. Think what you and I have had to say about it, and then imagine what the attitudes of the other parents would be. To say nothing of all the freedom fighters, law reformers, do-gooders and so forth. They'd spew out objections like gargoyles belching water from a church roof."

"Are you asking my advice, Hildidge?"

"If you care to give it, Sir Thomas."

"The Superintendent and his men have already worked wonders. You agree?"

"Absolutely. And I get the impression we haven't heard half of what they've achieved so far, even though they've only been on the job a bit more than a full day."

"Would we not then be right to assume that they should be able to continue the good work and will arrive at the final answer without recourse to even considering taking the fingerprints of the girls?"

"I think we would. I have every confidence in them."

"In that case, in view of the distaste that they themselves have expressed at the prospect of taking the girls' prints, why should we expect them to subject themselves to the public opprobrium that a request for parental consent would—according to you—call down upon their unfortunate heads? They have come here to tell us that they have succeeded thus far, but that there is now a choice of ways ahead. One distasteful and one requiring skill to negotiate. They have given you the facts and put themselves in your hands. Why should you hesitate to suggest that they continue to use their skill?"

"The only snag, Sir Thomas, is that the distasteful way would—were the consents forthcoming—prove entirely successful. And that's what Mr Masters is here to produce—success. Despite his skill, there can be no guarantee that the second road will lead to success."

"I take your point. May we ask Mr Masters for his view?"

"We would prefer not to ask for consents, sir."

"Excellent."

"But we will none of us guarantee success."

"Though we're pretty sure we can bring home the bacon," added Green.

"In that case," said Hildidge, "no request forms. Do it your way, Mr. Masters. And having decided that, let us have coffee before facing the rest of a bleak morning's work."

It was while he was helping himself to milk that Masters said to Hildidge: "Your daughter—Helen, isn't it?—must be about the same age as Sir Thomas' granddaughter."

"They are in the same form."

"Are they friends?"

"I suppose they are friendly enough, but not close friends. I mean, they don't go about together or visit each other at home as far as I know. Helen's closest friend is a little thing called June Hall."

Sir Thomas, standing close by, said: "June Hall? The architect's daughter?"

"That's the one, Sir Thomas. I was just telling Mr Masters she is a close friend of Helen's."

"So she is of Rachel, I think. I know Rachel brought her round to my house on one or two occasions in the summer. My cook made fools of them. Gave them strawberries and ice cream for tea in the kitchen and they repaid her by bringing in a baby hedgehog one day. I went in to see what all the screams were about. The maid was standing on a chair bawling her head off."

"Kids!" said Hildidge. "Still, who'd be without them?"

"I'm expecting to become a father myself," said Masters. "It's a long way off, yet. We've just got to know."

"Congratulations."

"The rain's stopped," said Green, joining the group, "but it still looks as if David had another bucketful or two to send down."

"Will that hamper your investigations?" asked Kenny.

"Not so's you'd notice, Sir Thomas. But it all depends what His Nibs here has in mind. If he's going to ask me to plod round Bramthorpe looking for laburnum trees I'll have to get my wellies out."

"A lot of gardens have them," said Hildidge. "I've got one."

"So have I." Sir Thomas wrinkled his brow. "And I'm pretty sure Norman and Barbara have one."

"The forensic man at the inquest said they were commonly grown. But they seldom grow wild, apparently."

"Golden Rain!" said Kenny sadly. "Nice name for a deadly tree, isn't it? It doesn't seem right somehow."

Masters put his cup down.

"Well, gentlemen, if you'll excuse us . . . We'll report again, very soon, I hope, Mr Hildidge. I want to work as quickly as possible, because the school breaks up for half term tomorrow."

"Good luck," said Sir Thomas. "Come and see me whenever you like."

"Now," said Masters, turning to Green as soon as they were in the car, "you said we'd bring home the bacon. So we'd better start looking for a few pigs and a tub of salt."

"Get out of it," said Green, taking out a battered packet of Kensitas. "You've got your ideas."

"True. The school key, which you lifted from Sir Thomas last night, will have to be tested."

"It was. At two this morning," grumbled Reed.

"With what result?"

Reed said: "I don't know yet, Chief."

"I thought you said you'd tested the white key fob."

"I dusted and photographed it, Chief. But I haven't got any further than that. There were two sets . . ."

"Distinctly different?"

"I'd say so, Chief, but I was so bog-eyed I just left them."

"I see."

"Sorry, Chief."

"Don't worry. I forgot I'd asked the D.C.I. to pick up the key. I'm gratified he remembered it after our talk last night. I certainly hadn't expected you to get so far."

Green said: "You're being magnanimous, George. Even complimentary. I would say that means you picked up some snippet in there from either Sir Tosh or Hildidge. While you were having coffee, was it?"

"Yes. Rachel Kenny and Helen Hildidge are not close friends."

"Would you expect them to be? Same class at school but different class outside. Hildidge was probably pounding a beat when his girl was born—with a police whistle in her mouth. While the other one would have a whole canteen of silver cutlery in hers."

Masters was by now too accustomed to Green's remarks of this type to rise to it as he once might have done. He took out his pipe and started to fill it, determined by his silence to force Green to ask for further information. At last—

"Well, it's interesting. Rachel and Helen aren't palsie-walsie. That should get us a long way. No wonder you're feeling pleased with yourself."

"Go on, Chief," suggested Berger. "There's more to it than that."

"Quite right. Though they are not friends they have one mutual friend who, it appears, is pretty close to both of them. The girl's name is June Hall . . ."

Both Reed and Green uttered exclamations when they heard the name.

"The punishment book," growled Green.

"Detention," said Reed. "I noticed last night she was two down and one to go according to Miss Bulmer's arithmetic."

"Quite," said Masters.

"So what?" asked Berger.

"As yet, nothing," said Masters. "Two girls are each friends of a third, but not friends of each other. We are looking, we think, for three girls. That's all."

"Come off it," growled Green. "You told me to pinch that key . . ."

"Right. The kids we want had to get into the school. There are plenty of keys to the secretary's entrance. Miss Holland gave every governor one each. But the only governor with a child—or grandchild—at the school is Sir Thomas. Because he uses the key so rarely, he leaves it in the drawer of the telephone table in his hall, so that he doesn't have to carry it about with him. It wouldn't be beyond the bounds of possibility for his little Rachel—on one of her frequent visits to his house—to borrow that key."

"You know what you're suggesting, George?" said Green grimly. "If it turns out that his granddaughter was instrumental in killing the woman he was going to marry, it'll break Kenny into little pieces."

"I realise that. But what can I do about it? This is a perfectly bloody case. You see, Bill, I can't get it out of my head that Rachel and June Hall are apparently as thick as thieves, and that June Hall is a prankster—as shown by the fact that she was either the instigator or at least party to the idea of introducing a baby hedgehog into the Kenny kitchen, to the consternation of the staff."

"When did you get to know that?"

187

"Over coffee, when we were chatting about the girls."

"Chatting? It may have seemed like chatting to them, but you were probing like a mad dentist."

"True. I couldn't get it out of my head that young Rachel was the girl with the best opportunity to get a key to the school. And then June Hall's name came up. Like you I'd made a mental note that she had appeared in both the punishment book and the detention book. The only one to do so within the last six months or so. So I already knew she misbehaved in school—to a serious degree, if what we are told about Miss Holland vetting punishments is true."

"I can't see why it shouldn't be."

"Right. And she obviously did bad work, too, otherwise she wouldn't be in the detention book."

"In short, she's a right little raver."

"I must assume so. But I must also assume that she is intelligent, because what we heard from Miss Bulmer concerning detention . . ."

"That's right. If she was a dim kid, she'd be encouraged, not punished. She must be a bright kid who's skiving if her name's down twice."

"So, Chief?" asked Reed. "You're reckoning on June Hall as ring-leader, are you? With the Kenny and Hildidge kids as accomplices?"

"Not quite. That would be jumping the gun."

"But June Hall?"

"We've got to keep our eye on her."

The car turned into the hotel car park.

"Let's have a quick look at those prints," said Green. "In His Nibs' room if the chambermaid's finished in it. If not, in a corner of the lounge."

* * *

188

Reed looked across at Masters.

"The same, Chief," he said, putting down his pocket magnifier.

"What's that mean?" asked Green.

"It means that two good, clear prints I got off the key fob are duplicated in those I got off some of the drums in the kitchen."

"So little Rachel was in it, after all," said Berger.

"What are you going to do, George?" asked Green. "See her parents and ask to take her dabs? Or go ahead and see Sir Tosh and put it to him straight?"

"Neither," said Masters. He took out his pipe and started to fill it carefully. When he was ready to continue, he said: "You see, Berger, you are not necessarily right in saying that Rachel Kenny was involved. All we can say for sure is that one of the three who handled the drums also handled Sir Thomas' key. Oh, I know the probabilities are that it was Rachel. But suppose—on one of her visits to Kenny's house—June Hall had borrowed the key . . ."

"How would she know it was there?"

"Rachel would know her granddad had it, and little girls gossip. Or perhaps June Hall went to use the phone. Kids do, these days, all the time. She could have been standing there waiting for somebody to answer and—again as is commonly done—she idly opened the little drawer, or she was looking for a pencil . . ."

"No good, Chief. How would she know it was the key to a school door, as distinct from any old key to any old door in Kenny's house?"

"Ah! You've got me there, I'm . . ."

"Wait! Wait!" exploded Green. "Of course she'd know." He looked at Berger. "How many keys have you seen around that School House?"

"Quite a few, and . . . You're right. They were all on white fobs—at least . . ." He turned to Berger. "In Groombridge House there was a board in the hall—full of keys on white fobs. I remember now."

"Right, lad. I reckon every key in that school is on a white fob." Green turned to Masters. "Couldn't we ring somebody up? The secretary perhaps. She'd tell us. I think each one is fobbed with a white tag that will take a name or a number to identify it. It's the sort of thing a fussy-britches like Miss Holland would insist on. Then when she gave the governors their keys, she gave them fobs, too. Every girlie in that school probably knows which is a school key and which isn't."

"Thanks, Bill." Masters turned to Berger. "So what I said still stands. But it is immaterial. My point is that June Hall—or any other girl from the school if it comes to that—could have discovered and borrowed that key."

"And returned it?"

"Easy enough. 'Can I use the phone, please, Rachel? I just want to ring Mummy to tell her where I am.' Then, wham! The key is back in the drawer. Kenny won't have missed it, because he uses it so rarely."

"Ho, hum!" said Green.

"However, I still favour Rachel," said Masters, "for obvious reasons. And June Hall."

"How about Helen Hildidge?"

"We have no reason to suppose she was implicated, simply because she knows June Hall."

"You hope," said Green. "The trouble with kids is that clever young imps, like June Hall appears to be, can lead others astray. Kids who would never think of misbehaving—other than being a bit naughty—can be jeered or dared into doing something daft. And then, every so often, it turns out to be as serious as this. I'm no religious maniac, but I agree with what it says in the Bible about whoever leads kids astray—whether they're grown-ups or other young devils."

"Amen to that," said Masters. "But now, gentlemen, let's put our thinking caps on." He turned to the sergeants. "You two reported that the head girl . . ."

"Melissa Craig-Deller," said Reed.

"The same. She told you that Miss Bulmer had said some girls looked pretty sick when the news of Miss Holland's death was announced."

"The teachers supported it, Chief. Miss Fryer especially."

"When you told us, we took it as confirmation that all the girls held a great admiration for the head-mistress and were distressed by her death. What if the shock was due to the fact that they thought—or knew—they had caused her death?"

"Good thinking that, man," said Green. "That's one thing we can check up on. We can get the names from Miss Bulmer and then check with Miss Fryer that she saw the same people looking the worse for wear. Even if she doesn't confirm Miss Bulmer, it widens the field a bit, that's all."

"No," said Masters. "We would really like Miss Bulmer to give us names, including that of June Hall. If the Fryer was looking in some other direction and saw some genuine case of distress, we'd do better to ignore it."

"Why?"

"Because somehow or another, we've got to identify the owners of the prints on the drums. That means we have to get their dabs by what can only be illegal means. It will be difficult enough to get three sets. Getting six or more will be a harder task and consequently more difficult to achieve by stealth. Because, please remember, taking prints from three girls—if discovered—will attract as much unpleasant attention as taking them from three hundred, especially after it has been agreed that none shall be taken."

"Where does that leave us and our conscientious objection to involving kids? We're as guilty if we do it clandestinely to a few as we would be if we did it openly to three hundred," said Berger.

"Not a bit of it," said Green. "If we get those dabs without those kids knowing, we won't be involving them. Our objection is to lining them up for a grisly enterprise. If we don't line them up and they know nothing about it, we'll have done them no harm. There's no humbug in that. It means we'll have gone out of our way and put ourselves to a lot of extra work to shield the little darlings from participating in normal police routine. But we'll also have done our jobs. That way everybody should be satisfied in every way."

"That says it all," said Masters. "So for heaven's sake, watch your step. No overt moves to get prints."

"That's all very well, Chief, but how are we to get them?"

"I can't tell you. I think we'll have lunch . . ."

"In a pub," interjected Green. "Not here. I want a pint from the barrel in a tankard, not a bottle in a toothmug."

"Just as you like. After lunch we'll try to get the girls' names from the Misses Bulmer and Fryer. Then we'll know whom we have to go after. That fact alone will make the task seem a deal easier."

They left the hotel. As they got into the car it was again raining and the wind had begun to gust strongly.

"Take us to some place where we can get a decent meal," said Green to Reed. "None of your Ploughman's on a day like this."

"Go where you like," said Masters, "but don't take too long about it. Remember the school breaks up for half term tomorrow morning. So we've only twenty-four hours before they spread themselves all over the country. And as I've no wish to go chasing after them, I'd like to make the effort to clear up before they finish."

"Quite right," said Green. "Besides, we need our weekend, too. I'd like to watch Chelsea tomorrow afternoon."

"Home match?"

"They never win if I'm not there," said Green airily. "I have a good effect on them."

"You can't have been attending very often this last year or two, then," said Berger. "They've not been exactly the most successful side in the country."

"Team-building, lad. It goes in cycles. We'll bounce back. And talking of bouncing, I'm being rattled about here like a pea in a pod. Take it easy over the potholes, Sergeant."

"The Chief said to look sharp."

"Not at the expense of life and limb."

"Never mind, we're there now. Sergeant Berger and I earmarked this pub yesterday. It has an air about it."

"It's not air I want," grumbled Green as he got out of the car. "It's Real Ale I'm after, followed by a big wodge of beefsteak and kidney pud."

In the event he had the dish of the day—liver and bacon—and rushed through it so quickly that the others were hard put to keep pace.

"To the school-secretary's entrance, please," said

Masters. "We should get there just before afternoon classes begin."

As they started away, Masters said to Green: "By the way, I forgot to tell you earlier, but Wanda phoned Doris yesterday to tell her about the baby."

"Did she say how Doris received the news?"

"Absolutely delighted."

"I knew she would be. We shall be knee-deep in knitting at our house for the next nine months."

"Wanda also sent you her love."

"I should think so, too. Here! Wait a minute! When did you call her?"

"It was too late last night after we'd finished talking, so I rang her this morning, just before I came down for breakfast."

"You what? Hadn't you heard that early morning is the worst time for a lass who's infantising? And you go and phone her before she's out of bed."

"She was feeling perfectly well. She said so."

"Of course she did."

"And she sounded it. Cheerful and pleased to hear from me. Besides . . ."

"Yes? Besides?"

"I asked Wanda for some information, and she was very happy to give it to me."

"What information?"

"You know she's very good at flowers and gardens and such like, where I am hopeless."

"Yes. Come to mention it, I can't see you planting the salvias and watering the azaleas."

"I wanted to know about laburnums. They flower—or so we've been told—in about June. Then the fruit comes—like peas in pods. But this is late October and I can't think that those drums were interfered with all that long ago. So what happens to the seed pods be-

194

tween June and mid-October? I simply asked Wanda if she could tell me."

"And could she?"

"She helped a lot. She reckoned that by mid-August the seed pods still on the trees would be drying out. Losing their pale, green, glossy surfaces and beginning to get rough and yellow."

"Just like peas, Chief," said Berger. "They then shrink over the fruit inside and you can see bumps . . ."

"We know what happens to peapods," said Green. "It's laburnums we're talking about."

"Wanda said the drying-out process would take about two or three weeks and then hulls and seeds would be dark brown like the seed pods on Russel lupins, broom and sweet peas."

"So that by the middle of September at the latest, laburnum seeds might be mistaken for peppercorns—in artificial light by somebody in a hurry and who's been unwise enough to assume that small, brown, spherical seeds in a box marked black peppers are, in fact, black peppers."

"Quite."

"And that means somebody had a month in which to plan and carry out the job."

Reed slowed to turn right through the big double gates of the school.

"Chief," said Berger, "do you reckon it was planned to use laburnum seeds, or did whoever did it just happen to notice them on the tree or fallen to the ground and think what a good idea to use those as well as the paint powders and plaster?"

"I think the former, because the two sets of substances are so different. I can understand paint and plaster because the girls will use them in their art classes. But laburnum seeds . . ."

"You may not have noticed," said Reed. "But we've arrived. We're there. Journey's end has been reached."

"Don't get sarky, lad," said Green. "It ill becomes you when even Sergeant Berger can inform us that dry pea pods show up in bumps and blains, and you can't even tell us whether laburnum seeds will give a cow that eats them the staggers."

"I tell you what I can ask you, though."

"What's that?" asked Green.

"It's been puzzling me, too," said Masters before Reed could reply to the D.C.I.

"What has?" asked Green.

"How the kids who planted that stuff in the kitchen knew they were going to annoy Miss Holland rather than Mrs Gibson."

"How the devil did you know that was what I was going to ask, Chief?"

"He knew because it's so obvious that only a bone-head like you would bother to ask it, lad," said Green without waiting to hear any reply from Masters. "I think that the answer to your question, however, must be that they thought that any action that would discommode Mrs Gibson would automatically involve or harass Miss Holland."

"And if it affected the boss-woman herself directly, so much the better?"

"Right, lad."

Reed didn't seem satisfied. "Are you satisfied with that, Chief?"

"I think I've got to be. Think of the alternative. The exchange of ingredients would have had to have been made on Tuesday, after Mrs Gibson's departure, if they were not to affect her."

"That would be easy to do, Chief. While Miss Holland was out shopping at the chemist's."

"Quite. But are you suggesting that the people who put those laburnum seeds in the pepper drum knew that Miss Holland would decide to cook Steak au Poivre that night?"

"Not unless she always did on Tuesday nights, Chief."

"We can't accept that she did. If Miss Holland was in the habit of cooking peppered steak, a woman of her intelligence would not have needed to consult the recipe book, which she patently did last Tuesday."

This argument silenced Reed.

Masters opened the car door and stepped out. The others followed him and they made their way—a posse of four big men—towards the school door.

Miss Freeman had obviously seen them coming through her office window, because she had the door open before they actually reached it.

"Good afternoon, Miss Freeman."

"Good afternoon." Miss Freeman made no attempt to stand aside to let them enter.

"I would like to see Miss Bulmer, please."

"I will see if Miss Bulmer is available." Miss Freeman started to close the door on them, but Green got his body in the way before she could do so.

"Hang on a moment, love. What's got into you? It's raining out there."

"Miss Bulmer has forbidden you to enter the school and has told all the staff, whether academic, clerical or domestic, not to communicate with you."

"Has she indeed?" asked Masters quietly. "Then I think I had better see Miss Bulmer and remind her that her action makes her liable to instant arrest for preventing me from doing my duty and you, Miss Freeman, the same, if you don't stand aside."

"Arrest? Me?" gasped the secretary. "What for?"

"Interfering," said Green. "It's quite a serious charge, love. Particularly in a serious case." He eased the door fully open. She backed away before him. "Now, off you go and tell your boss that my boss wants to see her pronto. And no messing."

The startled woman left them standing at the junction of the corridors and fled the short way to the little passage that served the suite containing the head's school study.

"We should have followed her," growled Green. "There's opposition mounting here. I don't like it. It's mounting everywhere. Sir Tosh's daughter-in-law, Sir Tosh himself and Hildidge, and now the school. We're going to find it hard to get the dabs we want, George."

"I don't like it myself, but we'll keep cool, even though we'll play it as if we're angry."

Green eyed him keenly. "Are you up to your tricks?"

"Not so's you'd notice. But if they think they're besting us, we'll play along. Let them think they've got our measure."

"If you say so. Me, I'd go for threats."

"Would it pay with Miss Bulmer? She's a cool, calculating mathematician."

"She'd still not like the idea of a few hours down at the local nick."

"I take your point. We'll play it as the opportunity arises. Threats if need be and they look like having some effect. Agreed?"

Green nodded and turned to the sergeants. "One of you keep an eye on this secretary bird when she comes back. No phone calls or trips around the school to warn people."

"Got it," replied Berger.

"You, Reed, stand by to act as messenger. We may want somebody to ferret out Fryer."

Reed nodded and turned as Miss Freeman came to rejoin them at an ungainly trot.

"Miss Bulmer says she can afford Superintendent Masters two minutes."

"Can she?" said Green. "We'll see about that."

All except Berger moved towards the study. Miss Freeman put out a tentative arm as if to stop them. Berger took her elbow and said: "Leave it, love. You come along to your office and make me a cup of tea."

"I said I would receive Superintendent Masters only." Miss Bulmer was cold and distant in her manner: totally unlike her attitude of the night before in the School House.

"I don't take orders, Miss Bulmer," replied Masters. "Not when I am engaged on police business."

"You do on these premises. I said I would see you merely to inform you that this school is a private institution. As such, police are only allowed on the premises by invitation. As temporary head of the school I am now withdrawing my permission for you to enter any building belonging to Bramthorpe College."

"Wrong," said Masters. "Wrong on two counts. You may be the temporary headmistress, but the authority for the school is vested in the Board of Governors and I have the permission of the Chairman of the Board to go and come as I please. That's the first count. The second is that once invited onto premises in the gathering of evidence for a case, that invitation lasts throughout the length of the case and cannot be revoked at will. In fact, Miss Bulmer, I would be within my rights to instal a permanent duty officer within the building until such time as I was satisfied that his presence was no longer needed."

"Very well. What do you wish to see me about?"

"To ask a simple question or two. On the morning that you announced to the assembled school that Miss Holland was dead, you were heard to remark that certain of the pupils appeared seriously shocked. Please tell me the names of those girls."

"Rubbish."

"You mean you didn't notice that certain girls were visibly shocked?"

"I mean I cannot give you their names."

"That is not very helpful."

"It was not intended to be."

"Is this deliberate non-cooperation, Miss Bulmer?"

"You can take it as such if you wish. But I would point out that the number of girls seriously shocked by the news was so great that the list would contain half the names in the school."

"I think your answer has no more than a veneer of truth, Miss Bulmer. Young people do not react quite so severely, quite so quickly to serious news unless it affects them so intimately as to precipitate shock. But we will leave that for the moment. Miss Fryer, your games mistress and, I believe, first aid expert, noticed a case of shock, too, though she misread it as a fainting fit which would probably need her attention. She will remember the name of the girl concerned and those companions who rallied her. I propose to send Sergeant Reed to fetch Miss Fryer if you will kindly tell us where she is to be found."

"I forbid you to approach Miss Fryer."

"Don't be a fool, ma'am," said Green. "How can you forbid a witness to speak? It's illegal and, I might remind you, attracts severe punishment in the courts."

"Don't try to frighten me, Mr. Green."

"I'm advising you, love, not frightening you. That would be as wrong of me as your attitude is of you."

"Miss Fryer is not in the school," said Miss Bulmer to Masters. "As there are no more games or gym periods before tomorrow lunchtime when we break up I gave her permission to go off for half term early."

"Are you trying to tell me," asked Masters, "that Miss Fryer teaches no subject other than gym, and that every week she has Friday afternoons and Saturday mornings free?"

"I am telling you nothing except that Miss Fryer is now on her way home for a week."

"Thank you. Now my last question, Miss Bulmer. Last night we got on amicably enough. Why has your attitude now changed so drastically that you are being positively obstructive? I say positively advisedly, because I believe you have been less than truthful with us, and I also believe that you granted Miss Fryer extra leave so that she would not be available here for questioning. Further, you have tried to deny us entry to the school."

"Mr Masters, when I first met you last night, I was not aware that you were trying to implicate girls from the school in a murder charge. It was only after I left you and I came to review the business of our meeting that I came to reailse what your investigations were likely to do. They would involve Bramthorpe in a major scandal. A scandal that could ruin the school. And for what? I do not believe that any girl here is implicated. But before the courts establish that, the damage will have been done. As headmistress of Bramthorpe I am not prepared to sit idly by and see the school suffer because of your blunders. Nor will I allow any of the girls who are now my responsibility to be harassed by police who are so patently on the wrong track. I intend to see that you change your area of investigation and that Bramthorpe College does not receive any publicity that would blemish its name. That is my duty and my intention."

"Some speech, love," said Green in mock admiration.

"Please do not refer to me as love."

"Have it your way. But I'll give you another word of advice. If you try to stop us doing what we've got to do you'll create such a stink that the publicity will rock the foundations of this school."

"There will be no publicity. There will be nothing to publicise. And, furthermore, I still have the right to complain of your conduct."

"Of course you have," said Masters. "I will give you the names of the senior officers to whom to complain. First off, locally, there's Chief Superintendent Hildidge and then at Scotland Yard there's . . ."

"My complaints will be made to members of the Government. Through its former pupils, this school has connections in places slightly more influential than the police hierarchy."

"Has it indeed! Well, Miss Bulmer, let me give you a quid pro quo. Start to do anything along the lines just suggested, and we, too, will have our say. In fact, I should have no compunction in recommending—because you are going to such great lengths to impede me that you must have something to hide—in recommending that you, yourself should be arrested for murder."

Miss Bulmer sprang from her chair.

"How dare you threaten me!"

"Please allow me to continue. The charge may not stick, but the arrest would be publicised, and I think I could make out so plausible a case against you that . . ." Masters stopped in mid-sentence before continuing more slowly, ". . . that the newspapers would have a field day and quite a lot of the mud would stick."

202

He finished talking and turned to Green. "A word with you. Outside, Bill."

"What about me, Chief?" said Reed.

"Stay here please, for the moment."

"What the hell's got into you, George?" asked Green when they were out in the corridor. "Threatening her like that . . ."

"You told me to, remember."

"Not to threaten to charge her with murder."

"You saw her reaction."

"Oh, yes, I saw it. I thought she was going to fling a book at you."

"Touched a sore spot, did I?"

"And how! But she'll call your bluff, that one."

"That's what I thought—at first. And then when I said I could make out a plausible case against her, an idea suddenly came to me. How we needn't worry our heads about those fingerprints."

"I saw the idea come. What was it exactly?"

Masters spent two or three minutes telling him. Green paid close attention even though during the recital he took out a battered Kensitas packet and lit up a cigarette. When Masters had finished speaking, Green paused reflectively for a few moments before replying and then said: "Why not? Let's try it for size. What's the first move?"

"To get Sir Thomas to agree to fix a meeting for us. He'll be present, of course. His son and Rachel, with June Hall and her father. I'll go and see him to persuade him it is absolutely vital. I'll take Reed. Can I leave it to you to question Miss Freeman and Miss Lickfold?"

"Right. When do you want this meeting?"

"This evening. Early. I'll try and get Kenny to lay it on for cocktail time—use a drink as the excuse."

"Right. What about Miss Bulmer?"

"We'll leave her. I'll just go and tell her we're leaving, and just to make her happy I'll say we shall probably have to tackle Fryer at her home. That'll please her."

He returned to the study.

"Sorry about that, Miss Bulmer. I've just sent one of my men over to Groombridge to get Miss Fryer's home number. I suddenly realised whilst I was talking to you that I could get it from there. Now, where were we? Oh, yes! You are still determined to be obstructive and you are going to report me. That being so, I think no further value is to be got out of this interview. So we will go, but we may well have to return, as I cannot leave matters in their present unsatisfactory state." He turned to Reed. "Will Berger have had time to get to Groombridge yet? You see, I don't want Miss Bulmer ringing through there to order them not to give him the number."

"You needn't worry, Superintendent. He won't get it. All the school staff—and that includes domestic staff—have been warned to refuse to speak to you."

"I see. So it is stalemate, Miss Bulmer. A great pity! This could all have been settled so easily and amicably. I hope you realise what a terrible position you have put yourself in, and your staff, too. I may well have to invite them to the police station to question them, and that can be a far from pleasant experience."

"My staff will follow my lead for the good of the school, Mr Masters."

"I admire loyalty, Miss Bulmer. But this could be sadly misplaced. However, you've taken your stand, so now we will go, to leave you to think things over."

When they had left the study, Reed said angrily: "She thinks you're stupid, Chief."

204

"She may be right. But not for the reasons she thinks."

"What was all that flannel at the end about anyway?"

"I wanted to lull her suspicions while the D.C.I. asked Miss Freeman a question or two and got the answers out of her before Miss Bulmer could intervene."

"Was that why you told her you were hanging on until Berger could reach Groombridge?"

"Yes. Come on now. If the D.C.I. has finished, collect him and Sergeant Berger and come out to the car. We've got a lot to do."

When they were all in the car, Masters said: "Stop at the first phone box. I'll see if Sir Thomas is at home. If he is, you can take us there. Then Berger can take the D.C.I. on to Miss Lickfold's house. You shouldn't have long to wait there, Bill, because afternoon school will soon be over, and I should think Lickfold hurries home. After that you can pick us up again."

"Right."

Sir Thomas must have been watching out for them at half-past six, for he opened the door before Masters had time to ring the bell.

"All here," he said. "And I've taken the liberty of inviting Hildidge. I hope that is agreeable to you?"

"Certainly. In fact, I'm pleased he is here. I have no wish for anything to appear hole-and-corner about this meeting."

"I hope not. You've really told me nothing of what you are about, and though I agreed to get Hall and his daughter here, I had a devil of a job to persuade him. He is not, you see, a friend of mine, accustomed to coming here. We are the merest of acquaintances, and a somewhat mysterious invitation to drinks at this time puzzled him mightily, and so he started to ask questions. In the end I had to fall back on what he took to be an ulterior motive, and confess that I wanted to sound him out concerning the feasibility of developing some property of mine. I'm afraid he is in for a rude shock, isn't he?"

"I think he will be grateful to you."

"I hope so."

"His daughter is here?"

"She was a stumbling block. He couldn't see why I should invite a schoolgirl to a business meeting over a drink, but she's here. I think cupidity finally triumphed over curiosity."

"Good. And Rachel?"

"Getting her—and Norman—was easy enough. He wants to apologise to you by the way."

"Please tell him not to bother. Now, Sir Thomas, if we could join the others?"

"Right. The girls are in the kitchen eating fruit cake. There is no prep tonight, so they feel they are on the spree."

"Good for them," said Green, following Sir Thomas into the drawing room. "That'll put on a bit of weight that in five years' time they'll be doing their damnedest to take off."

"Gentlemen," announced Sir Thomas, "the team from Scotland Yard. Everybody knows everybody except, I think, Mr Nicholas Hall. Mr Hall, Superintendent Masters, D.C.I. Green . . ."

When the introductions were over, and all had drinks, Sir Thomas said: "Gentlemen, Mr Masters has something he wishes to say, so would everybody find a seat, please."

"Fetch the girls," Masters whispered to Reed.

"Now, Chief?"

"Straight away."

"Well," said Hildidge heavily. "What now, Mr Masters?"

"Just a moment, please. We have two other interested parties: Rachel and June. The young ladies are just finishing off large slabs of fruit cake, I understand."

"What's June got to do with this?" demanded Hall. He waved one long arm around. He was tall and thin and, though scarcely in his mid-forties, gave the impression of a rather lugubrious senior citizen.

"Quite a bit, but nothing serious," replied Masters. "She and Rachel have been rather made use of, I fear . . ."

At that point the door opened and two fourteen-year-old little beauties came in. Rachel was fair, June was dark, but they wore identical jeans and T-shirts which showed off their budding figures admirably. They had the clear skins of youth, and the wide eyes of knowing and well-informed innocence. They had been enjoying themselves in the kitchen, and their attitude suggested they intended to go on enjoying themselves in this gathering.

"Sit down, please," ordered Masters. "The floor will do. Where you are, in the middle of the party."

As the two girls sat, Masters turned to look round the men. "I would appreciate it, gentlemen, if, despite any strong urge to the contrary, you would not interrupt what we have to say. This is by way of being a social gathering, but I think you will find it to be of significance to all of you. Your co-operation will be of value."

Without waiting for the several replies, Masters

said: "I'm going to tell you a story of failure—on my part—which I hope will turn out to be an eventual success. In Sir Thomas Kenny's hall is a telephone table, with a small drawer in which he keeps a key to the secretary's door of Bramthorpe College. Last night, I borrowed that key . . ." Masters held up his hand to silence Sir Thomas who was about to expostulate, ". . . I borrowed the key and, from its white, pear-shaped fob, my sergeants lifted the fingerprints of what they guessed was an immature young woman."

Green put his hand on Rachel's shoulder as she seemed about to speak.

Masters continued: "On a shelf in a kitchen unit in the School House kitchen we discovered several cardboard drums, the contents of which had been removed and replaced by inedible substitutes." Masters looked at the girls. "We found the fingerprints of immature young women on those drums, too, and to our great surprise, one set on the drums matched the specimens we found on the key fob."

This time there was no holding the outbreak from the men, but Masters refused to be drawn, and held up both hands until he once again had silence.

"No you may wonder why I lifted Sir Thomas' key. The answer to that is simple. Very early on we were of the opinion that a girlish prank was beginning to loom large in our investigations. I, therefore, made it my business to know which girls in the school were related to a keyholder, and I discovered that there was only one such girl. And that was you, Rachel. So I had to test that key. I could have been unlucky. But I wasn't. There were the prints of a girl's fingers and those prints coincided with some of those from the drums."

Both girls were watching him with fierce attention,

and even the men had lapsed into a state of unblinking concentration.

"Now I knew that the most likely girl to have touched that key would be Rachel. But I was told that June sometimes came to this house, so it could just be that June had left her prints on it." He turned to June's father as the latter spluttered angrily. "Please don't take on, Mr Hall. As police officers we must attempt to see every possibility. Were we not to do so, you—if you were not so intimately involved—would, quite rightly, condemn us for dereliction of duty. As it is, I am doing you the courtesy of letting you know our thought processes and I have already confessed to being mistaken."

Masters took his pipe from his pocket and a brassy tin of Warlock Flake. After he had opened the tin and selected a leaf of tobacco, he continued: "As I think I now know, that key was not used for entering the school premises, but you will admit that I had a right to believe that it had been so used in view of the same prints appearing in Miss Holland's kitchen." He looked down at the girls. "Please tell me which of you handled the key and for what reason."

Rachel said: "It must have been me. I knew where it was kept and I rummage a bit when I'm here, you know. Grandad never minds as long as I don't interfere with anything serious."

"Thank you. So shall we say that your prints were also among those on the drums of flavourings?"

"I suppose you must." She turned to June Hall. "We should have worn gloves. All the best burglars do, and we . . ."

"Please!" interrupted Masters. "Don't go on like that. You are causing great distress. I think it would be better if you just answer questions very briefly. We

DOUGLAS CLARK

now know you entered the School House and enjoyed
yourselves at Miss Holland's expense. Now, tell me,
was it at mid-morning break on Tuesday that you
went into the house, through the unlocked connecting
door?"

"It was," said June. "But how did you know that?"

"Young desperados like you should realise that even
some of us older ones can guess you would choose a
day when—because it was common knowledge—you
knew Mrs Gibson would be away. You also banked
on the fact that Miss Holland took her mid-morning
coffee in her school study."

"Always," said June.

"Not quite always," said Masters. "She returned to
the house during Tuesday morning break and discovered you two young ladies, didn't she?"

"It was rotten luck," said Rachel. "We kept watch
and saw her go to her school study as usual."

"But she let you down. Never mind. Just think back
to the time when you saw her go into her school study.
Was she alone?"

"No. That's why we were sure she would be there all
through break."

"Let me guess. Miss Bulmer was with her?"

"That's not a guess. The Bull told you."

"I assure you she didn't. Why should Miss Bulmer
tell me she took coffee with Miss Holland last Tuesday?"

"No reason, I suppose. But the Old Dutch did catch
Rachel and me in ... what's that Latin word? ... *flag*
something or another."

"Try red-handed, poppet," said Green. "I always
do. It's easier."

"Yes, thank you. She caught us red-handed, so she
was sure to tell the Bull when she went back to the

210

school study, wasn't she? She wouldn't keep a thing like that to herself."

"Thank you." Masters turned to the assembled men. "June has made an important point, which I should like you to note very carefully, gentlemen." He again addressed the girls. "How did Miss Holland react when she caught you?"

"Jolly well," said Rachel. "She was a bit shaken at first, of course, but when we confessed what we were doing, she laughed. I think she was in a bit of a hurry. She'd come back to get some papers and wanted to rush back to her coffee and the Bull, but she said she would talk to Mrs Gibson about it, and Mrs Gibson might want us to spend our next free afternoon in her kitchen cleaning up."

"She was serious about what she said?"

"No, I don't think so, was she, June? I know I felt jolly foolish. As I say, she was in a hurry, and she made us pick up our packets and she made us walk out in front of her."

"Like naughty schoolchildren, in fact?"

"I suppose so. But you could tell she thought it was a hell of a joke."

"Rachel!"

"She did, Daddy. She was trying to be serious and nearly bursting herself with laughing."

"That will do."

"Yes, Daddy."

"Now," continued Masters. "I had fixed on Rachel because of the key—a fortunate error on my part. And I had selected June as an accomplice not only because she was a close friend of Rachel, but because I detected a motive for June's involvement."

"Oh!" said young Miss Hall in dismay.

"Sorry, sweetie," said Green. "It's got to come out."

"I suppose so. But with Daddy here . . ."

"Your father won't get cross," promised Masters. He looked at Hall sitting glumly across from him. "There are two punishment registers in the school, in which are entered every misdemeanour that warrants any form of disciplinary action. The punishment book is for naughtiness—talking in class, playing tricks on the teacher or whatever it is our future matrons get up to in their form rooms. The other one is the detention book, and in this are entered the names of girls who are kept in school and given extra tasks for backsliding in their work. It is not intended for those who genuinely find difficulty or who try hard and fail. These are rewarded by encouragements. But the scapegraces who skimp their prep and get a delta minus when they are capable of getting an alpha plus are frowned on. Indeed, they are jumped on heavily. Such poor work attracts detention. But there is worse to come. Miss Holland was, quite rightly, so intent on girls realising their full potential and, thereby, raising the academic standards of the school, that even one detention in a term for any one girl was serious enough to earn a reprimand. Three detentions in a term could result in the parents of the girl involved being asked to remove her. In other words, Miss Holland reserved her right to weed out skrimshankers."

"Quite right, too," said Sir Thomas. "I agree with upholding standards."

Masters smiled. "Our young friend June here might not readily agree with you, sir. She appeared in both books. A Miss Corkadale had occasion to punish her for smuggling into a form room what is described in the book as 'a rude-noise maker' and proceeding to operate it to what I imagine can only be described as the detriment of good order and scholarly discipline."

"The Crocodile has no sense of humour," said Miss June Hall. She looked at Rachel. "It was jolly good, wasn't it, Raitch? Nice and loud and fruity."

"June!" Her father sounded despondent.

"And," continued Masters, "Miss Hall appeared twice in the detention book for gross dereliction over History and English written prep."

Miss Hall looked faintly abashed.

"I therefore imagined," continued Masters, "that June had been in hot water and that Miss Holland had warned her that she was near the edge of the precipice. Am I right?"

"Oh, absolutely. She gave me a wigging. Said she was considering what course to take. To ask Daddy to remove me or to send me down a form until I bucked my ideas up. That I think was what she had decided, and that would have been a stinker because they're all such goons in that form that I would . . ."

"Don't go on," said Masters. "We know what your feelings were, and we can guess that to pay Miss Holland back for the stand she was taking you decided to play a practical joke on her."

"I say," said Miss Hall, looking up at Masters with large, beautiful and seemingly innocent eyes, "you are an understanding sort for a member of the fuzz, aren't you? I thought you were all piggy."

"Thank you for the compliment." Masters looked across at Hildidge. "So I had opportunity—wrongly arrived at; motive—from the punishment books; and as for means . . . Well, I suppose anybody can go to an art shop and buy paint and plaster. That meant I had the three essentials of a case against these young ladies. However . . ."

"Shouldn't all this be brought out in court?" asked Hildidge, plainly uncomfortable that the workings of

213

the police should be thus paraded before the lay public.

"If you recall, sir, only this morning you asked me to solve your case without recourse to fingerprinting and the involvement of too many of our young friends in police business. Unfortunately, these two were vital to the business, so I did the best I could. I avoided police stations; I invited their fathers to be present, while you and Sir Thomas are here to see fair play. This way, we can avoid courts—at least for the time being."

Hildidge shrugged to show he gave reluctant approval for Masters to carry on.

"Rachel and June, who else did you take with you into the School House kitchen?"

"Nobody. We told you. The Old Dutch found just the two of us."

Masters looked across at Hildidge. "I have already informed you, sir, that we discovered three sets of prints that shouldn't be there. So, strange as it may seem, there must have been two separate visits to Mrs Gibson's kitchen that day. One by Rachel and June. One by another person. Please note that this is so great a coincidence that I cannot accept it as fortuitous. I believe the second visit came about as a direct result of the first one having taken place."

Green grunted to show he was fully in accord with this belief.

"Now," continued Masters, again addressing the girls, "please tell me exactly what substance you took with you into the kitchen and substituted for the wholesome foodstuffs you found there."

"A packet of the plaster stuff we use for modelling with in art, and some packets of paint powder."

"That is all?"

"Yes."

"You are absolutely positive you took nothing else in there with you?"

Both girls swore they were telling the truth.

"Very well," said Masters. "Which one of you nearly fainted in Assembly on Wednesday morning?" It was a shot in the dark, but it found its mark. "I did," whispered June Hall.

"Why?"

"Because . . . because I'd got Raitch to help me and it wasn't her fault. But it was mine."

"What was?"

June remained silent.

"You thought Hiss Holland had eaten something that you had taken in and that she had become ill and had died, didn't you?"

June nodded miserably. "At first, yes."

"And it shocked you so much you nearly fainted?"

"Yes."

"You said 'at first'. What happened to change your mind?"

"It was Rachel. She said Miss Holland had seen exactly what we'd done and which drums we'd refilled, and she wasn't the sort of juggins who'd forget and then use them. In any case, she wouldn't be able to eat sauce made with plaster because it would set hard and if she'd used the paint powders the food would have been an awfully funny colour. She wouldn't have touched it. And even if she had forgotten we'd been there, she'd soon have remembered when she saw red stew or something, wouldn't she?"

Masters nodded.

"And then," said Rachel quietly, "we heard Miss

Holland had been poisoned with laburnum seeds and we'd not taken any of those in. I don't think I've ever seen laburnum seeds."

"Nor me," said June. "So it really wasn't our fault, was it?"

"No," said Masters, "it wasn't your fault. But people who play practical jokes and who get caught by the police get short shrift. Do you understand?"

Both girls nodded.

"Right. Detective Chief Inspector Green is going to think up some punishment for you. Now."

"That's right," said Green as they turned to him. "It is half-past seven and I missed my tea and now I'm missing dinner. By eight o'clock, I want—in here—a plate of good ham sandwiches with mustard, made by you yourselves, and a large pot of coffee. I've no doubt some of the other gentlemen here will have similar orders for you to execute. So ask each one. Make a note of them and then skedaddle. And I want everything in here at eight o'clock prompt. Not before. Not after. Got that?"

"Yes, sir."

"Right. Sharp's the word now."

Green had hit the right note. As the two girls scrambled to their feet there were signs that all those present were beginning to relax. And while the chastened pair went round prettily asking what people would like, Sir Thomas enlisted the help of Reed to replenish the glasses.

"Had you got that food business laid on?" asked Hildidge as soon as the girls had left the room. "It looked rehearsed to me."

"I had asked Bill Green to get rid of them on some pretext at that point if I gave him the hint," admitted

216

Masters. "You can trust him to come up with some practical and satisfying exercise at such a time."

"I felt sorry for the kids," said Green. "They're a couple of little ravers in my opinion. I wouldn't have minded having a pair like that myself. It's natural that bright lasses like that should get up to practical jokes—I'd rather they did that than smoked pot and indulged in illicit sex. Besides, Miss Holland could see the funny side of it. She'd probably done much the same thing herself when she was young, because from the looks of her she'd be just such another as those two are when she was a choker. And then, after the Old Dutch, as they call her, had taken it so well, she went and died. No wonder your June nearly fainted, Mr Hall. And it was good thinking on young Rachel's part to pull her round, Mr Kenny. So I take it you two gentlemen will not make the mistake of blaming them for what came after?"

"No, no, of course not," said Hall.

Norman Kenny said: "I just thank heaven they weren't responsible."

"Good," said Masters. "Shall we continue? We had established several things which caused us to reconsider the whole affair. Our situation was: if not the girls, who then? Whose were the third set of fingerprints?"

"What drum were they on?" asked Hildidge.

"On the drum which contained the laburnum seeds was a third, single set of prints, different from the several sets we found on the drums containing plaster and paint. As I am assuming the girls told the truth, I must also assume that the prints on the drums containing plaster and paint are theirs."

"A fair assumption," agreed Hildidge.

"Let me tell you what we think happened, and the steps we have taken so far to prove our case. Further proof may be necessary, but only to tie up loose ends.

"Miss Holland returned to her school study where she was entertaining her deputy to morning coffee. The girls tell us she was amused at their prank rather than angry. My belief is that Miss Bulmer saw the amusement on the head's face and asked the cause of it. I've no doubt Miss Holland told the story with some relish and in such great detail that the mathematical mind of Miss Bulmer could visualise the whole scene exactly.

"As the conversation over coffee developed and touched on different subjects, as always happens on such occasions, I believe Miss Holland to have mentioned that she was going to have a quiet afternoon and evening. All she had to do was to make a trip to the chemist for a few bits and bobs for her holiday and after that prepare her own supper, using the piece of steak Mrs Gibson had brought in for her. At this point I think she probably said that she wished she knew some way of preparing steak other than grilling it or frying it as she did every Tuesday.

"My next supposition is that it was at this point that Miss Bulmer saw her opportunity. I believe she said: 'Why not try Steak au Poivre?' Miss Holland asked how this was prepared and Miss Bulmer replied: 'It's bound to be in Mrs Gibson's cookery book. Look it up. It really is very easy.' To this Miss Holland must have replied: 'I'll do that. I'd like to try my hand at something new.' " Masters paused a moment before going on. "We know Miss Holland did consult the cookery book that day, because the page which held the recipe for Steak au Poivre was marked by an envelope franked the day before and, therefore, only received by her last Tuesday."

"Go on," growled Hildidge. "This is getting interesting."

"The knowledge that Miss Holland intended to visit the chemist was vital to Miss Bulmer. It meant the School House would be empty but easily accessible through the unlocked connecting door. Miss Freeman, the school secretary, has informed us that though Tuesday afternoon is a games afternoon and, therefore, no classes are held in the school, Miss Bulmer was on the premises from soon after lunch until after four o'clock."

"You are saying she sneaked in and put laburnum seeds in the pepper drum?"

"I believe she watched for Miss Holland to leave and then, armed with a new pepper drum which she had filled with laburnum seeds, and which she had been careful to handle only with gloves on or with a handkerchief round it, she exchanged the drums, leaving her own and come out with Mrs Gibson's."

"If she handled it with gloves on, how did she get a third set of immature female prints on it?" demanded Hildidge.

"That's the bit that had me foxed for a moment, sir, until I remembered that check-out girls in supermarkets are often immature females. We know which supermarket this came from, because the price ticket is peculiar to that particular shop—a shop, incidentally, which Mrs Gibson swears she never uses. We shall have to take a few dabs in that shop to confirm our theory."

"Anything else?" asked Hildidge.

"Yes. I must hurry or those two little girlies will be back. Miss Lickfold whom, I think, Miss Holland rightly moved from her post of deputy headmistress, nevertheless has convinced us that some of the reports reaching Miss Holland concerning Miss Lickfold's shortcomings emanated from Miss Bulmer. Some untrue. There are other mistresses to support this and they all agree that where they would try to cover for a colleague, Miss Bulmer was intent on putting the skids under her. The result was that as next senior mistress she became deputy head. I believe that to have been her first step. That exercise took her three years. The next step, were she to follow the same tactics, she knew would never succeed. Miss Holland was too strong and successful ever to be ousted in similar fashion. Besides, time was not on Miss Bulmer's side. She was an older woman than Miss Holland and so, were they both to continue normally, Miss Bulmer would retire first. Only in the event of Miss Holland's death could Miss Bulmer hope to attain the headship of Bramthorpe College. And so Miss Holland had to die."

"Do you mean she had an overweening ambition to become headmistress?" asked Hall in an astounded voice.

"Yes, Mr Hall, I do. And she reckoned that once she had been appointed deputy head by a woman of the calibre of Miss Holland, the Board of Governors would find it difficult to refuse her application should the job of headmistress become vacant."

"Quite right. We would," said Sir Thomas.

"Today," went on Masters, "I think Miss Bulmer lost her head. On the pretext that she was guarding the good name of the school and in the interest of the girls, she went so far as to forbid all staff—domestic as well as academic—to talk to us, and to refuse us entry to the school and its buildings. She seemed to us to be so fiercely determined to protect Bramthorpe now that she is acting head that it caused us to look much more closely at her. We wondered at her attitude. She had become proprietorial concerning the school. And I remembered one little thing that struck me as odd last night. Without really looking into those drums, it was she who identified the contents as paint powder. A maths mistress knowing about paint powder . . . ? Well, maybe. But I reckon she knew because Miss Holland had told her over coffee last Tuesday morning."

"Is that it?" asked Hildidge.

"Except for bits and pieces. Are we right?"

"Of course you bloody well are. It's as sweet as a nut. When shall you arrest her?"

"After school breaks up tomorrow, if that suits you."

"That'll be best."

"No, gentlemen," said Green, "can we change the conversation, please? Our two little totties should be on their way."

A moment later a clock in the hall started to chime. On the first stroke of the hour the door opened and two girls pushed a laden trolley in.

"How's this?" June asked Green.

"Just the jobbo."

"We did try to find two of the maid's old mini skirts, but she had no black stockings and suspender belts so we gave it up as a bad job."

"You," said Green, "don't need any aids like that. Either of you. Mr Masters is married to a grown-up version of you two, and she's the berries. I could almost believe she went to Bramthorpe as a kid. She's got the same air about her."

"She did," said Masters. "She's a Bog. She often laughs about it."

"Bog?" demanded Green amazedly.

221

"Bramthorpe Old Girl," chorused the two young misses.

Green was outraged. He tackled a ham sandwich like a lion taking a tasty joint at feeding time. Sir Thomas drew Masters aside. "If only she'd waited a few months, she would have had everything she wanted."

"But would she have been the right one, Sir Thomas? Considering what we now know about her?"

Sir Thomas shook his head sadly.